A Greek Misadventure

Elaine K Collier

PEACHY PUBLISHES

For Mum

Who taught me that life is for having as much fun as possible. You will always be with me.

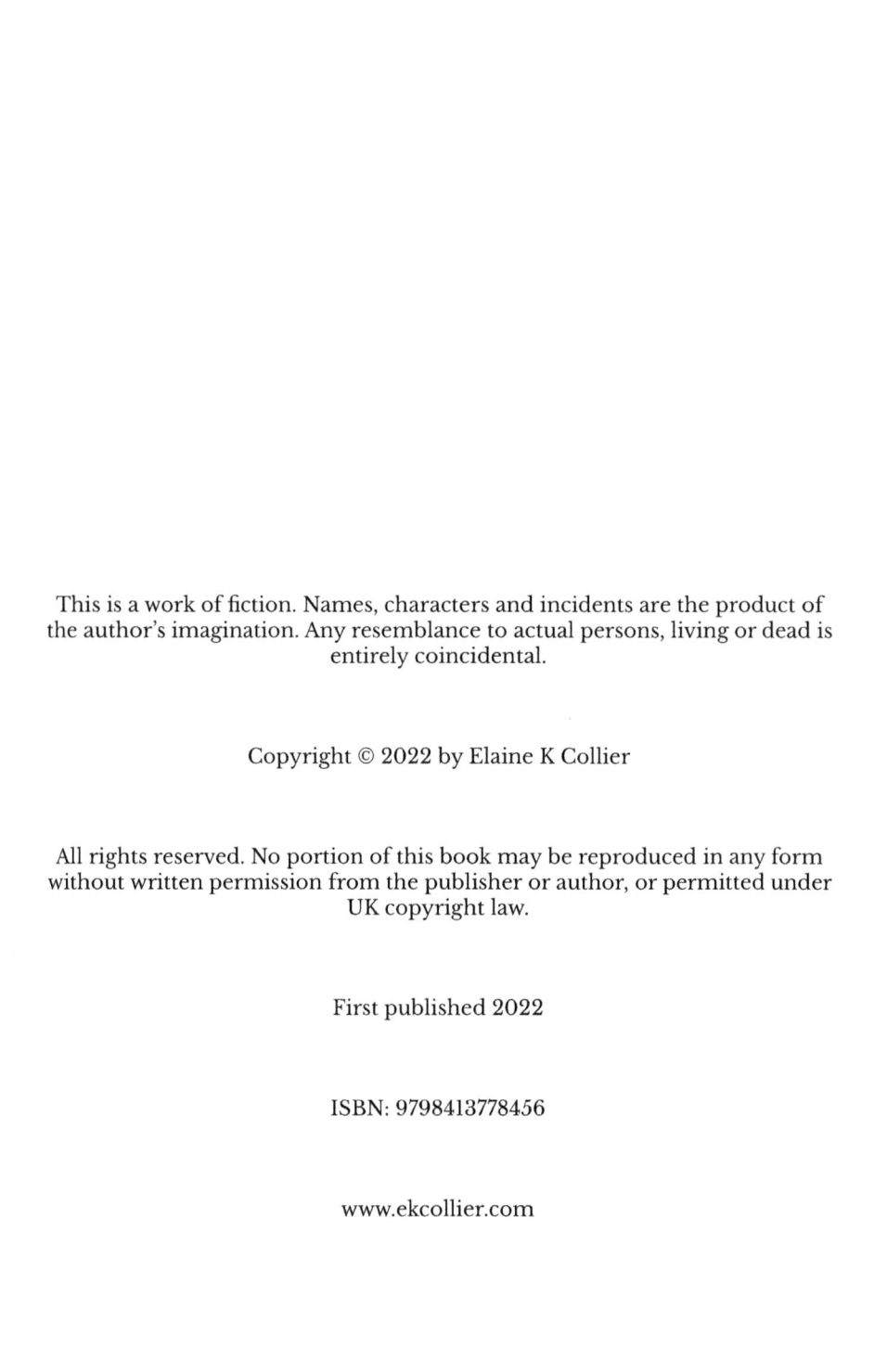

This is a work of fiction. Names, characters and incidents are the product of the author's imagination. Any resemblance to actual persons, living or dead is entirely coincidental.

Copyright © 2022 by Elaine K Collier

All rights reserved. No portion of this book may be reproduced in any form without written permission from the publisher or author, or permitted under UK copyright law.

First published 2022

ISBN: 9798413778456

www.ekcollier.com

ALSO BY

Also by Elaine Collier

Once Bitten, Twice Prepared

The Bigger Picture

Free short stories – The Man, Reflections and Closing the Ring – are all FREE to download from www.elainecollier.com.

Chapter 1

"Morning, love, how you doing?"

"Oh hello, Donna, I was just thinking about you," smiled Fiona.

"Ah, synchronicity strikes again! Just thought I'd give you a ring cos I want to ask you something. Dave and the boys have gone off to football training so I've got a couple of hours free and making the most of it."

"Sounds serious, should I be worried?"

"No, I'm hoping you'll like it."

"OK." Fiona was intrigued.

"I've been thinking."

"Oh, steady on. That can lead to trouble."

"Mmm, yeah, I know, but listen. It's our big birthdays next year and we haven't been on holiday together for ages so I just wondered whether you fancied going somewhere to celebrate the big five-oh?"

Donna was excited, she had been considering a holiday with Fiona for ages, if she didn't suggest it now she would miss the moment. A week or two lazing about in the sun with her best friend would be wonderful and with their big birthdays looming, it was the perfect occasion.

"Oh, I don't know," replied Fiona, "I'll have to ask Jeremy."

"Sod Jeremy, he's not bloody coming and what's it got to do with him anyway?"

"That's harsh, Donna, you know he always likes me to run everything by him first."

"Yeah, he's always been a bloody control freak. You shouldn't have to do that, you've got a mind of your own, at least you used to have. If you don't want to go on holiday with me, then just say."

Donna felt irritated. She wanted her friend to say yes, not run it by sodding Jeremy, pompous twat that he was.

"Of course I want to go on holiday with you. It would be wonderful. Look, can I let you know tomorrow?" Fiona asked.

"Yes, OK, I suppose so. But don't take any nonsense from him, make your own mind up. Just tell him you're going, end of story. OK?"

"OK, I'll call you tomorrow. Love you."

"Love you too, babe, speak tomorrow."

Donna ended the call and sighed. Fiona had taken all the excitement away from her. A week in the sun would be wonderful with some precious time together. Not if sodding Jeremy had his say they wouldn't. What the hell had happened to Fiona. She never used to be so bloody downtrodden. *I'll have to ask Jeremy, my arse*, thought Donna. She used to always make her own decisions. What had changed? she wondered.

They hadn't been on holiday together for quite a few years. It wasn't anyone's fault; it was simply that life got in the way. Donna thought their birthdays would be a fabulous opportunity to start them off again. She missed the time alone with her bestie, the long conversations, sharing a drink or several, dancing till dawn, laughing, even doing nothing other than just being together. Oh, she loved Dave and the

CHAPTER 1

boys to pieces and there was nothing she wouldn't do for them, but she also missed time on her own with Fiona. Fiona didn't put any pressure on her. She didn't constantly ask to do something or go somewhere. They took each moment as it came. All Donna wanted was some time to herself now and then, time where having fun was her main aim. Time without being someone's wife and mother. Was that too much to ask?

Oh well, nothing more she could do now except wait. Banging around in the kitchen, Donna made a coffee and took it outside. Her garden was her sanctuary, it soothed her soul. Lush and fresh with the smell of last night's downpour still lingering in the air, the vibrant green shrubs enhanced with the pinks and purples of the summer blooms. The sound of water running down into the fishpond calmed her. When the weather was fine, she spent as much time outside as she could. This morning she wanted to make the most of being home alone for a couple of hours and enjoy some peace and quiet in the late summer sun before she had to leave for work. It wouldn't be long before the colder, darker days of winter set in and she wouldn't get the warm sunshine she craved. Spring and summer were her favourite seasons, winter was just a time to get through. Thank God they had Christmas to break up those long, dark, tedious months.

She let out a long wistful sigh. She really hoped that Fiona agreed to the holiday.

Chapter 2

Fiona ended the call with Donna, not really knowing how she felt. She loved chatting to her best friend, but this morning had left her in a bit of a quandary.

She hadn't expected Donna to suggest a holiday. It had been years since their last one and she thought those days were long gone. Jeremy had made such a song and dance about her going last time that she never suggested it to Donna again. Anyway, Donna was always off with Dave and the boys and, to be fair, Jeremy took them to some wonderful destinations every year, so she couldn't really complain at all.

But she missed those fun times with Donna, times where she could totally let her hair down and be herself. Donna never judged her. That was the beauty of having her as a best friend. Donna accepted her for exactly who she was, and she knew her better than anyone else ever had or ever would. Jeremy had expectations and she was constantly on her guard in case she let him down. Sometimes she found it easier to say nothing, convinced that people felt there was no substance to her. Her family holidays were not so much about fun, but more about culture and what money could buy. As soon as her children were old enough they stopped going away with Mum and Dad, much preferring to go off with their friends, and who could blame them. Holidaying with Jeremy alone was worse than staying at home. He set a daily itinerary and she was expected to trail round after him for a whole three weeks.

No, if truth be told, a holiday with Donna was exactly what she needed to bring back the sparkle of Fiona Johnson again. The thought of a week or two away filled her with joy and brought a smile to her face, but the thought of having to broach the subject with Jeremy filled her with dread.

Fiona knew Jeremy would forbid her to go. Over the years he had turned into a selfish man who wanted everything done his way and he expected her, and the children, to fall in line. Her life with Jeremy had become stale and boring, and the sad thing was he had no idea how she felt. She wondered if he even cared.

No, she had to make a decision, and it was going to disappoint either Donna or Jeremy. Would she take the easy option and keep the peace, or would she do something for herself for once?

Oh decisions, decisions!

Chapter 3

Fiona Johnson and Donna Edwards met thirty-odd years ago at university. Each had left it far too late before applying for accommodation in the halls of residence and ended up sharing a large, terraced house together with with three other students. It worked out well though as the two of them were drawn to one another and clicked immediately.

Their housemates were a real mixed bunch, two guys and a girl, all likeable in their own way, but it was Fiona and Donna who hit it off from the word go. There was something about each of them that appealed to the other.

The first thing Fiona noticed about Donna was her smile, it reached her eyes and lit up her entire face. An inner glow seemed to radiate from her that was difficult to ignore. She had a great sense of fun and a thirst for life. Donna laughed a lot, and wasn't self-conscious about anything. She was easy to talk to and always up for a good time. Donna brought out Fiona's fun side and she blossomed as their friendship deepened. She had never known anyone quite like Donna and found it totally refreshing. She knew her mum wouldn't approve, especially with Donna's propensity for swearing, but her dad would love her.

Fiona hated the end of term holidays when she had to go home and spend time with her overbearing mother. She loved both her parents very much, but she missed Donna and the fun they had together.

Donna felt she had known Fiona forever, even though they had only just met. There was a calmness and serenity about her, and Donna always felt at peace in her company. She loved that they could talk for hours about anything and everything, even burble on about nothing when they'd had a few drinks. They had a similar taste in clothes, music, books and even men. Fiona instilled some common sense into Donna and taught her to think things through rather than diving straight in. She had a calming influence on her. Donna knew that meeting Fiona was one of those things that was just meant to be.

As complete opposites their friendship should never have worked, but they brought out the best in one another. A lifelong friendship was born. They became almost inseparable and could always be found at the centre of social events on campus, mostly in a bar somewhere. Their sense of humour and laughter a magnet to others.

Sitting in the student union bar one Wednesday night listening to the mounting excitement of their housemates, Donna and Fiona came up with a plan. The boys were off backpacking around Europe for the summer and Donna felt it shouldn't be exclusive to the guys. She wanted to feel that same sense of eager anticipation and to experience different parts of the world and cultures. Fiona wholeheartedly agreed and so they devised a list of places they wanted to visit and planned their own trip, their first summer holiday together.

They got jobs in a local bar and saved their earnings. Porker, a big pink china pig, took pride of place on Fiona's dressing table and they dropped all their loose change into it. Less likely of the two to raid Porker for a good night out, Fiona took on the role of guardian. It was surprising how quickly the money mounted up. They cut down on spending as much as they could and survived on just the essentials. Fiona's parents were great, especially her dad who often sent her a little extra money, which went straight into Porker. Although Donna's mum protested about the amount of groceries disappearing from her cupboards, she always stocked up with Donna's favourites when she knew she was coming home.

CHAPTER 3

Both sets of parents felt it unsafe for their girls to go off traipsing around the world. Danger surely lurked around every corner, and Fiona's mother had visions of the girls being raped and pillaged by undesirable foreigners. But they had made up their minds and eventually left with a string of "don't do this and don't do that" ringing in their ears, all of which they totally ignored. They had such an amazing time and came to no actual harm, well certainly none that warranted telling their parents about, so did it all again the following year. Their annual holiday tradition was born.

Donna and Fiona's university days were some of the best days of their lives. Both came away with 2:1 degrees, Donna in nursing and Fiona in psychology. They could have done better, but their social life and having fun were much more important. They discovered a lot about themselves during those years, both strong, independent women who saw no end to the fun that life could offer.

The year they left uni they took off for the last time as students and travelled around the Greek islands. It was, by far, their best holiday, and it was there that their dream of sharing a flat together in London took shape. Donna knew she would easily get a job in one of the large London teaching hospitals and Fiona dreamed of a fabulous career with the London Metropolitan Police, solving nasty crimes.

But the practicalities of life after university kicked in. Living back in the family home saw their freedom curtailed as they were expected to comply with house rules. Fiona was in Oxfordshire and Donna in Cambridgeshire, too far away from one another to continue their social life. They needed to find jobs if their dream of London living was ever going to happen.

Donna got a job immediately at Addenbrooke's Hospital in Cambridge as a Registered Nurse. She enjoyed her work very much and had hopes that eventually promotion might come her way. She also enjoyed the social life. She made a lot of new friends and spent more time out of the house than in it.

Fiona found it hard to settle and eventually decided to continue her studies and specialise in Clinical Forensic Psychology for a PhD. She got a part-time job in Tipplers wine bar in Oxford during evenings and weekends to bring in a bit of money. Her parents were very good and expected nothing from her, her mother just thrilled that she had such a clever daughter and delighted in telling everyone that her Fiona had an 'ology'.

Fiona and Donna agreed to carry on as they were for the next few years and save any spare money towards the deposit on their new place in the big metropolis. But life often has a way of intervening and the best laid plans go tits up.

Chapter 4

"It's me and I'm coming." Fiona was full of excitement when she phoned Donna the following morning.

"Wow, that's bloody fantastic. Oh, babe, I'm so happy, we'll have the most amazing time just like when we were younger. Well, maybe not quite like when we were younger. What did Jeremy say?"

"He wasn't happy at all. In fact, he told me he didn't want me to go. But after you'd called yesterday, I started thinking about all those fabulous times we had and suddenly I really wanted to have some of those fun times back again. It was when he said I couldn't go that I just saw red and told him I was going and there's an end to it. We had an almighty row, of course, but do you know what, Donna, I really don't care what Jeremy wants."

"Well, good for you," said Donna, "it's about time you stood up for yourself and having some fun is long overdue."

"Where are we going?" Fiona asked.

"Oh, I don't know. I didn't really think about it too much in case you said no and, to be honest, I don't care as long as we're together."

The pair spent well over an hour talking about where they should go and when.

"May or June would be a good time, warmer weather and before the kids break up from school," suggested Fiona.

"Agreed. But where shall we go?"

"Oh blimey, I don't know," said Fiona. "They world is our oyster."

"You know what, Fi, the holiday I remember the most is Greece, we had so much fun there. So what about Rhodes? It has everything we need."

"Sounds perfect. But then I'm happy to go anywhere. Listen, Donna, I'm going to have to go. I've got a Ladies Lunch Club in an hour and I need to get ready." Donna rolled her eyes. Bloody hell, her bestie had turned into a *Lady What Lunches*.

"OK, leave it with me then and I'll do a bit of research on the internet and see what I can come up with."

"That's great. Sure you don't mind?"

"No, it's fine. You go and meet your *ladies* and we'll talk again soon. Fi, I'm so happy that you said yes."

"Me too, speak soon and love you."

"Love you lots too."

Still smiling, Donna made herself a cup of coffee, got her laptop, notebook and pen, and set herself up at the breakfast bar in the kitchen. She spent the next couple of hours googling her way round Rhodes. There were a couple of options, both all-inclusive, adults only hotels that had superb sea views, looked gorgeous and weren't overly expensive. She knew Fiona wouldn't have a problem with the cost, but she didn't want to spend too much on this trip as there would be less money for her holiday later in the year with Dave. She couldn't wait to get to Rhodes though, and wished it wasn't so long to wait until next year. In the meantime she would simply daydream about perfect days in Rhodes and let the excitement build.

CHAPTER 4

Donna loved her holidays, in fact, she lived for them. They had some fabulous family times when the boys were smaller, but now they were older they wanted to go off with their mates and not with Mum and Dad anymore. Their first family trip to Disney World in Florida when the boys were younger will be forever etched in her memory, especially when Tom, her youngest, insisted that ET knew him. He hadn't cottoned on to the fact that his name was programmed at the start of the ride so that ET could say a personal goodbye to everyone at the end.

Donna still loved going away with Dave of course, but it wasn't quite the same as being with Fiona and certainly didn't have the same level of fun and adventure and the *God knows what's going to happen next* element to it. That's what she craved more than ever right now. Perhaps it was because she was getting older that she felt the zest for life of her younger days beginning to dwindle. She knew that when she was with Fiona, she could hold on to that zest for a little while longer.

She sent a WhatsApp message to Fiona and included the links of the two hotels she had short-listed. They were adults only and fully inclusive, so no fear of being dive-bombed by kids in the pool and no big bar bill at the end of the holiday.

As soon as Fiona got back to her, she would make the booking. She only hoped that sodding Jeremy didn't start working on her friend in the meantime. She knew that if he kept on, he would eventually grind Fiona down and she would cave in again. Donna couldn't understand why Fiona put up with it. She knew she wouldn't let Dave, or any man come to that, walk all over her in the same way.

Oh well, she had to back off and let Fiona deal with her own relationship with Jeremy. She put it out of her mind as she took some bags out of the bottom kitchen drawer, grabbed her car keys off the hook by the back door and set off into town to do some grocery shopping.

Chapter 5

They bored Fiona stiff. She never liked these lunches at the best of times, but today her mind kept drifting. When she wasn't thinking about the holiday with Donna, she was thinking about the row with Jeremy the previous evening.

It was Jeremy's idea that she join the Ladies Lunch Club. The women were all wives of his colleagues. Each of them had undergone so much surgery over the years that they were probably barely recognisable from their former selves, with their look of permanent surprise and puffed-up lips. Talk about the Real Housewives of Oxford.

Jeremy was a consultant plastic surgeon doing NHS work at the John Radcliffe Hospital in Oxford but also ran a private clinic in Harley Street. Very status conscious, he had to have the best of everything, and that included his wife. He had suggested many times that he do some surgery on her, a little facelift, a tummy tuck, even breast enhancement, but Fiona always refused. He couldn't understand why. Surely any woman would welcome the chance of getting rid of some saggy skin, but he never thought of suggesting it to the big bellied, double chinned male colleagues around him. Typical man.

The Ladies Lunch Club met once a month at some fancy restaurant or other around town. There were five of them, excluding Fiona, all vying to be top dog. Fiona never felt she really fitted in with the group. They were acquaintances rather than friends. But she went along to the monthly lunches because it was something to do, but mainly to please Jeremy.

"Fiona, are you listening? You seem miles away. I asked if you and Jeremy were going to the Gala Ball next month?" said Annabel, probably one of the most reconstructed women she had ever come across. Everything was pointing upwards and Fiona often imagined all surplus flesh pulled tightly up to the top of her head and secured under her hair with an elastic band. The woman could barely open her mouth, let alone eat.

"Oh yes, sorry. Yes, I think we're going, but I'll need to check with Jeremy. Look, I'm so sorry, ladies, I'm going to have to dash off. I've got an appointment this afternoon and I don't want to be late, and you know what the traffic is like. I'm so sorry and I'll let you know, Annabel, if we're going to the Ball. Bye everyone." Fiona grabbed her bag from under the table and headed for the door.

She couldn't wait to get out of the restaurant. Their endless trivial and absolutely inane conversation was really doing her head in. She didn't have an appointment at all. She just wanted to get home and look at the hotels that Donna had pinged over to her on WhatsApp. Fiona was getting excited about the trip, despite the gloom that Jeremy had cast over the whole idea.

She let herself in the front door, disabled the alarm and kicked off her shoes. Like something straight out of *Ideal Homes* magazine, every room in her house was spacious and perfectly decorated in soft pastels. Jean, her cleaner, had already finished for the day, so everywhere was spotless and smelled fresh. Sunlight flooded through the floor to ceiling glass panels along the back wall. Fiona loved looking around her new kitchen. The total chaos and upheaval when the builders were there was certainly worth it in the end. The tri-folding doors onto the patio brought the garden inside and the muted tones of beige and cream with the odd splash of green gave the sense of continuous flow.

CHAPTER 5

Fiona switched on the kettle, popped her laptop on the island and fired it up. She made a cup of tea while she waited for it to connect to Wi-Fi and go through its initial procedure, and then perched on a stool. Sipping her tea she clicked on the links that Donna had sent. They both looked fabulous, but one really stood out. A white building, steps leading down to the road and golden sands and the turquoise colours of the sea beyond were stunning. She looked at all the photos on the hotel website and yes, of course, they were always going to look good, but she could just see herself and Donna lounging by the pool sipping cocktails. Spacious rooms with white walls, white tiles on the floors, and splashes of colour added here and there. It all looked clean and cool. The hotel had evening entertainment, which was always a bonus. It wasn't too far to walk into the Old Town of Rhodes, and she was sure they would find some wonderful trips to go on. Absolutely perfect!

She sent a quick message to Donna with her preferred option.

Nothing more she could do now but wait. Preparing the evening meal for her and Jeremy, she hoped he would be in a better mood after a day in his London clinic. The air was still very frosty that morning after the row the night before. Fiona didn't know what came over her, but when Jeremy said that he forbade her to go on holiday with Donna she suddenly saw red and told him she wasn't asking his permission, but was simply telling him she was going, end of story. He took himself, and a bottle of single malt, off to his study and that was the last she saw of him. She felt him get into bed much later, but she feigned sleep. She didn't want to start the whole thing off again.

CHAPTER 6

Donna had a fun-loving nature, she was probably born with it. As a child she was into everything, laughed easily and loved people. As a teenager she was popular and sought after by her schoolmates. Some might have called her wayward, but she simply lived for the moment and enjoyed the moment she was in. She swore a lot, smoked, and wasn't averse to the odd joint or two, and absolutely loved anything with an alcoholic content. Everyone loved Donna and she was never short of friends to have fun with.

She'd had her fair share of boyfriends and even a few one-night stands. She'd had her heart broken more times than she could remember and had broken a fair few in return. She believed in living life now rather than waiting for the right time, or right occasion. The zest for life never left her.

Donna married Dave Chambers around twenty-five years ago and she still loved him as much now as she did when they first met, maybe even more so. She was pregnant, twenty-four years old and, although totally in love, she wasn't ready for a baby. Many said it was inevitable that Donna Edwards would end up pregnant with her wayward lifestyle. Although she knew she ultimately wanted to marry and have a family, she was still too busy having a good time. She had a very full and active social life. She had Dave, her colleagues at work and she still went on holiday every year with Fiona, she really didn't want that to end.

She met Dave a couple of years earlier at one of the hospital discos. The brother of one of her fellow nurses, he had come along with his sister because he figured that with a room full of nurses he couldn't go wrong – his chances of pulling that night were high. And pull he did. His sister introduced him to Donna and they spent the rest of the evening together. He walked her home and asked if she would like to go to the cinema with him the following evening. She agreed and she fell in love. Her mum loved Dave from the start too and laughed much more when he was in the house.

Donna wondered how he would take the news of her pregnancy, but he was fine. Quite excited about becoming a father, he immediately asked Donna to marry him. As she leaned into his strong, muscular body and looked up into his twinkly blue eyes, Donna knew that she would always be able to lean on him and feel totally protected.

Dave was a sub-contract builder and had a reasonable income. Between the two of them they managed to put down a deposit on a small terraced house and furnished their first home together. Gavin was born a few months later, and they both idolised their baby boy. Two more boys, Mark and Tom, followed and Donna settled into motherhood surprisingly well. Looking after her family plus her job as a nurse, which she went back to a few years after Tom was born, meant she had very little time for herself. Her parents and her sister helped when they could, but all-in-all life was fairly hectic. Her annual holidays with Fiona gradually gave way to family holidays and, although she missed her friend very much, Donna couldn't be happier.

She often wished Fiona lived closer, so they could see a lot more of each other. Dave and Donna had been to stay with Fi and Jeremy in Oxford a few times, but to be honest, it wasn't great. She didn't much care for Jeremy; he was pompous and looked down on her and Dave. She knew Dave didn't like him at all and only went to keep her happy. The entire time spent there was stressful, and they had to work hard at being nice and sociable. Fiona and Jeremy had visited them once at their home in Cambridgeshire, but that was even worse, and they never went again.

CHAPTER 6

Donna missed her friend. She was the one person who she could be herself with, could talk to about anything, could tell her anything and knew it would never be repeated. She had never found that same level of friendship with anyone else, and neither did she want to. Fiona really was her best friend. She wasn't about to give up on that friendship and hoped that their upcoming holiday would rekindle the deep bond they shared.

Chapter 7

"We're booked!" Donna was so excited she could hardly wait to Facetime Donna the next morning.

"Fabulous. Is it the hotel we wanted?" asked Fiona. She hoped it would be as it looked lovely on the website, and she could just see the pair of them swanning about in their swimwear, colourful floaty tops, wide-brimmed hats and enormous sunglasses – very Audrey Hepburn-ish!

"Yes, I paid extra for a room with a sea view and balcony, and also I extended the last day by a few hours so we could get showered and changed before we left for the airport. I hope that's OK with you?"

"Oh God, yes, that's perfect. Gosh, Don, I'm so excited. When do we go?"

"We fly out on the 5th May at 6.25 from Gatwick. It's a bit early, but I figured we'd be there in time for lunch and then we've got the afternoon to unpack and get our bearings before dinner and the evening entertainment."

Fiona couldn't hide the excitement she felt. That little spark inside her had been reignited, and she knew that waiting for May to arrive would be unbearable. She wished Donna lived closer so they could share their excitement together.

"I'll e-mail you all the details so you can see exactly what's what. Now, we can either meet at the airport that morning, or what about we go the day before and stay at a hotel next to the airport overnight? I know it will cost a bit more but it will save us getting up in the middle of the night."

"Yes, that's a great idea, let's do that. I'll get a lift, or just book a taxi. I'll do a bank transfer later for my half of the money."

"There's no rush, I trust you completely."

"Yeah, I know that," replied Fiona, "but I would sooner pay it now and then it's like I really am going."

"OK, love, whatever works for you. Great on the Gatwick hotel. Leave that one with me then and I'll book us a room. I'll get Dave to take me to the hotel, or maybe one of the boys will do it. Oh Fi, this is really exciting. I am so happy you said yes to going on holiday. By the way, how's things with Jeremy this morning?"

"Not great. I only saw him briefly before he left for the hospital, but he's barely being civil. I hope he gets over it quickly because it's going to be hell living with that until we go away."

"Yeah, well, don't let him spoil it for you. We'll make this the best holiday yet!"

Chapter 8

Fiona was the complete opposite to Donna. A pretty blonde baby with big blue eyes, she was quiet and well behaved. As a teenager she was reserved and spent most of her spare time with her head in a book. Although she had a few friends who she went out with occasionally, Fiona was basically a good girl and rarely got herself into any trouble. She was a people pleaser and would go out of her way to make others happy, often at the cost of her own happiness.

She worked hard at school, but her main love was sport. Being quite tall and slim, she seemed to be a natural and was one of the first to be picked in any team events. She ultimately became captain of the school netball team and they won most of their inter-school matches and competitions. She was made prefect and in her final year she made it to Head Girl. Her mother couldn't have been prouder and couldn't help but include 'head girl' whenever she talked about Fiona to her friends and acquaintances. Even the check-out woman in Waitrose knew about her Fiona.

It was a foregone conclusion that Fiona would go to university, get a good degree, and carve out a suitable career for herself, one that her mother would be happy with. What none of them bargained for was her meeting Donna.

Her friendship with Donna had been the making of her. Fiona had blossomed and she discovered a passion for just about everything that had been sadly lacking in her life. She found herself copying Donna in a variety of ways and loving every minute of her newly discovered freedom. She started swearing and loved the look on Donna's face when she dropped her first 'f-bomb'. She learnt to enjoy alcohol and the best ways to deal with the inevitable hangovers. The one thing she drew the line at, however, was the one-night stands. She needed to be in a loving relationship before she fully gave herself to anyone. Oh yes, Donna had a lot to answer for, and Fiona would be forever grateful to her.

After she left university, Fiona moved back home with her parents. She didn't want to but had little choice. She loved her parents dearly, her dad was a sweetheart, but her mum could be a bit much at times. Fiona was an only child and her parents doted on her. She knew they only wanted the best for her, but she found it suffocating. Her mum was so status conscious and more concerned with what people thought than how her daughter and husband felt. Her dad was lovely though, and she could wrap him round her little finger. She was totally a Daddy's Girl.

Her dream of sharing a flat with Donna in London was looking less and less likely, mainly because they'd spent all their money travelling around Greece during the summer after they graduated. She didn't regret that for a minute, they'd both had the time of their lives, but now her life at home with her mum and dad was totally boring. She missed Donna and their life together so very much.

She got a part-time job in a local wine bar, which brought in a little money, but mainly because it took her away from the house. But Fiona found it hard to settle and find the full-time job she wanted. Eventually, encouraged by her dad, she decided to continue her studies. Although she had a degree in psychology, she soon discovered that she needed more if she was to carve out a brilliant career for herself. Finally deciding on the path she wanted to take, she enrolled for a doctorate in Clinical Forensic Psychology, specialising in abusive relationships. Of course, the thought of her daughter being called Dr Johnson was another feather in her mother's cap.

CHAPTER 8

She enjoyed the three-year course very much and gained her PhD with relative ease. That was probably due to not having Donna around to lead her astray. With a PhD under her belt, she landed a job with Thames Valley Police and really enjoyed her work. Her role was mainly with abuse cases, from domestic to rape, and even the odd serial killer case. Life was good. She was earning money and still putting a lot of her spare cash into Porky even though the dream of the London flat had been put on hold longer than either of them had anticipated.

She met Jeremy at the wine bar where she worked. More crowded than usual that evening, noisy and full of smoke, Jeremy pushed his way to the bar to get in a round of drinks and made a beeline for Fiona. He was on a night out with a group of his colleagues and had to lean halfway across the bar to make himself heard. He was very chatty, and she quickly noticed that it was always him who bought the drinks, and he always came to her. His night out must have cost him a fortune. Towards the end of the evening, Jeremy asked if she would like to have dinner with him the following Saturday. She couldn't think of any reason not to, so accepted. They swapped phone numbers and were soon going on regular dates.

Jeremy was a junior doctor at the local hospital and doing rather well for himself. He wanted to specialise in plastic surgery and aimed to work his way up to a consultancy. His ambition was to open a private clinic in London as well as seeing private clients a couple of days a week in Oxford. He came from a wealthy family of surgeons and doctors so money had never been a problem, he always had everything he wanted in life. He thought Fiona was a splendid match. She was extremely attractive, tall, slim, with long blonde hair, blue eyes and, with a little tweak here and there, he would be proud to have her on his arm.

Fiona found Jeremy attractive, tall, dark and handsome, but then he knew it. Her mum was absolutely delighted and encouraged the romance with endless enthusiasm. Having Jeremy as a son-in-law really would be a major coup. The couple married a few years later and it was a rather grand affair. Donna was, of course, Matron of Honour, but she quickly picked up that if Jeremy had his way, she and Dave wouldn't have been at the wedding at all.

After the wedding and a wonderful honeymoon in Mauritius, the couple settled into their lovely new home in Jericho, Oxford. Their son, James, came along a couple of years later, followed by Lauren two years after that, and Fiona established her new life as a wife and mother. She had given up her job with the police when she had James, and Jeremy never saw the need for her to go back to her career. Financially, she certainly didn't need to. Her husband provided well for his family and gave her a generous monthly allowance, but she missed the work and camaraderie of her colleagues and the few friends she had made whilst working there.

Once the children started school Fiona found herself quite isolated and, if truth be told, lonely. She broached the subject of returning to her career several times, but Jeremy didn't want her to. Instead, he introduced her to the wives of his colleagues, hoping she would find a little niche for herself there, maybe pottering about with some charity work, but she never felt fully at ease in their company.

Oh, how she missed Donna. This holiday was really proving to be a lifeline for her.

Chapter 9

The beginning of May arrived before either of them knew it, and Fiona and Donna only had one day left before they jetted off to the sun.

"Right," said Donna during a Facetime chat one morning, "I've got the shower gel, toothpaste and suncream. Can you get the shampoo and conditioner cos I know you're fussy about what you put on your hair."

"Yeah, that's fine. I'm popping into town in a minute, so I'll pick them up. How many pairs of shoes are you taking?"

"What? For God's sake, Fiona, this is a holiday, not be a bloody fashion parade. I've got flipflops for the daytime and one pair of more blingy sandals for the evening. I'm taking one medium to smallish handbag, shorts, and T-shirts for during the day and two or three pairs of trousers, a few dresses, and dressy tops for the evening. Does that help? Remember, we have a weight limit here, it's not the first-class travel that you're used to with Jeremy."

"No, I realise that, Donna, I just want to make sure I don't over-pack but that I have enough for the two weeks."

"You'll be fine, Fi, and if you're not, then you can always buy it when we get there."

"Yeah, that's true. I've booked a taxi to take me to the hotel and I should be there by about two-ish. If I'm there before you I'll check in and take my bags to the room, then I'll wait for you in reception. Oh Donna, I'm so excited, it really will be like old times."

"Yeah, but not too much like those old times the last time we were in Greece, I hope," Donna laughed, as the memories came flooding back. "Remember, we're older now and supposed to be wiser, plus I don't think either of us could pull the all-nighters we did then."

"Yes, you're right. I'm usually ready for bed by around nine."

"For heaven's sake, some holiday this is shaping up to be."

"No, don't worry. I'll be fine when we get there. Promise."

"You better be, lady. Right then, I'll see you tomorrow at the hotel. Gavin's taking me, so I'll ask him to get me there for about two. Look forward to seeing you tomorrow, babe, have a good journey."

"Look forward to seeing you, too. Love you. Bye."

Fiona disconnected the call. Just one more night of looking at Jeremy's miserable face and then she was free for two entire weeks. Jeremy's mood had steadily deteriorated over the past week although, to be fair, he'd not been his normal self since she told him she was going on holiday with Donna whether he liked it or not, and nothing he could say or do would stop her. He really didn't like that she had developed a mind of her own and had tried everything he could to stop her from going off with Donna. He just couldn't understand why she would rather be with Donna, who, in his opinion, was clearly out of her league. She would be better off staying within their own circle of friends.

But right now, she didn't give a toss about what Jeremy thought. That little spark inside her was shining brighter, and she felt much better for it.

Right, better get off into town and then come home and start packing.

Chapter 10

Tuesday

The taxi appeared on the driveway on the dot of eleven. Fiona wondered if he'd been sitting round the corner waiting for the clock to tick over before coming up the drive. Jeremy had already left for the hospital and didn't even bother to wish her a happy holiday. Not that she expected him to, but it would have been nice. With no-one to say goodbye to, she set the alarm and shut the front door behind her.

The journey to Gatwick should really take less than a couple of hours, but the traffic nowadays was always an unknown factor. Fiona hated to be late when she went anywhere so, totally true to form, had given herself plenty of time and added on an extra hour, just in case. She didn't expect Donna to be there, but she didn't care. She was just happy to be out of the house and on her way to a fortnight's bliss.

She never thought she would feel this level of excitement again. It was very strong when she was younger and with Donna, but over the years of being married to Jeremy it had dwindled. It was wonderful to have that feeling back again. She felt so alive.

The drive to Gatwick was uneventful and her driver expertly manoeuvred his taxi around the traffic starting to build on the M25. Arriving at the hotel with an hour to spare, she collected her luggage from the side of the car where the taxi driver had placed it and headed for reception. The room wasn't ready. The cheery receptionist told her to try again just after two, but she could leave her bags in the room behind the front desk if she wanted to.

Fiona wandered over to the bar area. There were a few people here and there, but on the whole it was fairly quiet. She carried her cappuccino over to a seat by the window so she could have an unrestricted view for when Donna arrived. She knew she had a fair time to wait, but she didn't mind. She had loaded her iPad with new books the day before, so she had plenty to read. She couldn't concentrate. The people around her and her own thoughts distracted her. She was like an excited schoolgirl, and she was pretty sure Donna would feel the same.

"Mum," Gavin shouted up the stairs. "If you don't get a move on we're never going to make it for two."

"Coming, love. Can you just come and get my case for me, please?"

Gavin, her eldest, idolised his mum and would do anything for her, but she exasperated him at times. Everything she did was last minute and although she didn't seem to mind running around like a blue-arsed fly, it caused a lot of stress for everyone else. He'd readily agreed to take her to the airport, but he knew full well that it wouldn't be without its issues. *Thank God her flight is not until tomorrow*, he thought.

He loaded her bags into the boot of his BMW and virtually pushed her into the passenger seat so they could get going. According to Google Maps the trip should take a couple of hours but they were using motorways and there were always problems and roadworks. But Donna, in her infinite wisdom, had declared that if Google Maps said two hours, then two hours it would be. It was gone midday when they finally pulled off the drive so it would be a miracle if they made it in a couple of hours.

CHAPTER 10

There were a few roadworks around the M25, but Gavin finally pulled up outside the hotel entrance just after two. *Not bad*, he thought, *considering!*

Fiona came running out of the hotel, squealing and waving her arms in the air. Her delight at seeing them was obvious. Gavin got out of the car and walked around to give her a hug.

"Hello, Auntie Fi, you're looking as gorgeous as ever." He enveloped her in his strong, muscular arms and hugged her tightly. He had always had a soft spot for his Auntie Fi even though he didn't see her that often.

"Oh Gavin, such a flatterer. And look at you, when did you grow up to be so handsome?"

"It's in the genes, Fi, he clearly takes after me," said Donna as she flew out of the car and hugged her friend so tightly that Fiona thought she might cause an internal rupture.

"Oh, it's so good to see you, Donna, you have no idea how much I've missed you."

"Yes I do, because I've missed you too."

Wheeling his mum's suitcase into the hotel, Gavin turned and hugged them both.

"Have a lovely holiday you two, but stay safe and out of trouble," he said, and left for home.

Fiona and Donna linked arms as they made their way to the reception desk and the start of their long-awaited holiday.

Chapter 11

Wednesday

The girls had an early start the next morning, which was just as well as neither one had slept very much. Excitement kept them awake talking well into the early hours and now they were dragging their luggage along the inter-connecting corridor straight into the terminal for their 4:30 check-in. The big screen showed the number of their check-in desk and it didn't take too long to get to the front of the queue. With passports and ticket details in hand they checked in, said goodbye to their luggage and collected their boarding passes.

Security was painless too and neither of them got frisked, which was unusual for Donna. She always felt guilty at airport security and obviously looked it because she was always the one in the family to get picked on. She wouldn't have minded so much if it was a big, handsome guy but no, she got the short, grumpy woman.

"Right, Fiona, let's start this day in style and get some breakfast."

Checking out a few restaurants, they chose the least crowded and a waiter guided them to a table. Donna picked up the menu.

"OK, let's start this holiday how we mean to go on. I'm having Eggs Benedict, some toast, a cup of tea, and a cheeky little Prosecco while we're waiting. What about you?"

"Oh go on then, make that two of the same," said Fiona, smiling up at their handsome waiter.

While they waited for their food, they chatted about what they wanted to do while they were in Rhodes. Although they had both been before, it was many years ago and their memories were vague. Most of those memories were made under an alcoholic haze, so their accuracy was anyone's guess. A visit to the Old Town was a must, and Donna suggested a day trip to Symi at the very least. A trip to the acropolis at Lindos might be nice too but Fiona drew the line at a donkey ride to the top.

Pushing their plates away and draining the last of their drinks an hour or so later, they made their way out of the restaurant. They got caught up behind a group of young men causing a bit of a commotion by the door; at the centre of the group stood a unicorn. As the guys started shoving and pushing one another around they apologised for getting in the way and the unicorn asked if they would like to join them for a drink.

"Oh, we'd love to, wouldn't we, Fi?" Donna grinned at Fiona. Their holiday had started well and was beginning to be the type of adventure they were used to. Only Donna and Fiona could be invited for drinks in an airport at five in the morning by a unicorn.

The guys were off to Estonia for a stag do. Resplendent in a multicoloured onesie, complete with a horn stuck on his head, the groom had downed quite a few beers and was best friends with everybody. Full of fun and laughter and up for a good time their weekend was already looking like it would be a very messy trip.

Donna and Fiona spent a happy half an hour chatting away and enjoying another glass of Prosecco.

CHAPTER 11

"I've got a good idea," said one of the boys, "why don't you both come to Estonia with us? We could have loads of fun." The rest of the guys cheered and agreed they join them. That Donna and Fiona were twice their age didn't seem to matter at all, and the girls' egos lapped up the attention.

"Ahh, that certainly is a great idea, but we booked our holiday months ago so afraid we have to decline your invitation."

The girls finally made their excuses and left with a round of hugs and kisses and headed for duty free.

Faffing around cosmetics, as usual, Fiona was an easy target for the sales assistant and jumped at the chance of a make-over. *Typical Fiona*, thought Donna, leaving her friend to it as she headed over to the perfumes. She wanted to get some aftershave for Dave and the boys but, on reflection, decided to buy it on the way home rather than lug it about with her now. She couldn't resist, however, the beautiful perfume bottles of Jean-Paul Gautier and liberally sprayed herself from the sample of the torso of a woman in blue. Treating herself and Fi to one each, which came with a free handbag-size spray, she swiftly made her way back to cosmetics to chivvy up her friend. They needed to get a shift on if they were to make the flight.

Chapter 12

Once boarded, Fiona relaxed into her seat and let out a big sigh. Donna was struggling to get their hand luggage in the overhead locker when a steward appeared at her shoulder.

"Can I help you with that, madam?" Donna handed over the bag and collapsed into her seat.

"Phew, I hate getting on and off flights, it's always such a bloody crush of bodies trying to be first. I honestly don't know what the need to rush is all about, we're on holiday for Christ's sake."

"It's always the same," laughed the steward, "flying seems to bring out the worst in people, but then for some it can be quite stressful."

"I suppose so, but it's part and parcel of going on holiday and this plane is going nowhere until everyone's on board and strapped into their seats."

"I'll be back with the drinks trolley once we're airborne, if you're interested."

"Oh yes, we most definitely are." Donna tilted her head upwards and gave her best smile.

"Oh, for God's sake, Donna, what are you doing? He's gay."

"Really? How do you know?"

"Trust me, I know these things. So you can wipe that look off your face cos you'll get nowhere there."

"Well, I'm not here to get laid, Fiona! But he's lovely and has such a gorgeous face, I don't care whether he's gay, straight or mixed, there's just something about him and I think he's lovely."

The aircraft slowly backed out of the gate and made its way onto the tarmac. As the engines revved and the plane hurtled down the runway, Fiona put her head back and closed her eyes. Finally, they were off.

"You alright, Fi?" asked Donna, concerned that her friend might be feeling slightly sick after the early morning alcohol they had already consumed.

"I'm fine, Donna; in fact, I'm more than fine. You know, I've had visions of Jeremy turning up at the airport, creating a scene and making me go home with him. Now I can relax, he can't get to me while we're in the air."

"No, Fi, he can't and don't worry, I'm with you now and even if he turned up, he's not making you go anywhere you don't want to go. We're on holiday so let's forget all about home for two entire weeks and concentrate on having the best time ever."

Once the plane had levelled and the seat belt sign switched off, the steward started making his way down the aisle with the refreshments trolley.

"Here we are, my ladies," he said, as he placed their drinks on the fold-out tables and crouched down beside Donna. "So, where are you two staying?"

"The Majestic Palace near the Old Town, for two glorious weeks of sunshine, excitement and freedom," said Fiona, feeling that internal spark growing ever larger.

"Wonderful. I know that hotel, it has a great reputation," said the steward. "I'm lucky enough to be staying near the Old

Town with a friend for a few days and really looking forward to some relaxation and a bit of fun, too. I rarely get time to stay over but I haven't seen Demetrios for years so asked for some time off. Have you been to Rhodes before?"

"Yes, but many years ago when we were at university," replied Donna. "To be honest, the whole trip passed by in an alcoholic haze. I expect it's changed a lot since then."

"Not too much. Some new hotels have sprung up and it's probably a bit more touristy than you remember, but the Old Town always remains the same. Perhaps we could meet up one night and have a few drinks, maybe something to eat. I'm Matt by the way and it's lovely to meet two gorgeous girls who are clearly out to enjoy themselves."

Donna smiled. Bloody hell, they hadn't even reached Greece yet, and they had been invited to Estonia by a unicorn and now asked out for drinks by a gay guy. Woo-hoo, what next?

Donna agreed to meet Matt the following evening in the bar of their hotel and they swapped phone numbers. She felt drawn to him for some reason, but she didn't know why. Feelings of familiarity with someone she had just met had been with her throughout her life. Bit spooky really, but she just knew when something was going to happen, whether good or bad. The feeling that she got from Matt was like the feeling she had when she first met Fiona and look at how that had turned out. She was certain that this was the start of a wonderful friendship with Matt, and it would last longer than just the holiday in Rhodes.

"What on earth are you doing?" asked Fiona. "You don't know him from Adam. He could be a bloody serial killer and finish us both off in Rhodes."

"He's not and he won't," stated Donna. "I've got one of my feelings about him, he's going to be a fabulous friend and one that might come in very useful. Trust me."

"OK," said Fiona stiffly, "but don't blame me if he murders us in our beds."

"I wouldn't dream of it," replied Donna, smiling at her friend.

Donna lifted her glass and they both settled back and chatted away for the four hours it took to get to Rhodes.

Chapter 13

Matt was thirty-two and had been working as cabin crew for most of his working life, except for the odd couple of years he spent in a poodle parlour. Matt loved animals, they were much nicer than some people he knew, and he thought working in the parlour would be a brilliant start to a career with them. Turned out it wasn't.

For most of his life Matt had brought home a variety of animal waifs and strays, even a few who weren't, but his dad always made him take them back. He never got to keep the adorable ginger kitten that he kept in the garage for a few days whilst plucking up the courage to bring it into the house. The only one he got to keep was Reuben, a baby duckling that he rescued from a drain. Sadly, Reuben was dead by morning so it hadn't been an issue and maybe his dad had known that there would be no happy ending. He'd finally got Bounder for his twelfth birthday. An adorable but soppy golden retriever puppy who'd turned out to be his second-best friend. Joanne was his first best friend but only because he had known her longer. He guessed his mum had a lot to do with the arrival of Bounder and he was very grateful to her.

Matt met Joanne on the first day of primary school. He was standing alone in the playground and she sidled up to him and slipped her hand into his. Their friendship grew from there. Joanne was the only one who ever really understood him, except for Bounder of course. He could often be heard late into the night murmuring his secrets to Bounder. He knew he was different from the other boys, but he didn't know why. Joanne accepted him for who he was, even when Matt wasn't sure himself. He never had to pretend to be like the other boys when he was with her, and she never tried to change him.

Matt was not a stupid boy, he had a string of GCSEs and a foreign language and would have achieved a lot more too if he had engaged with school more. But Matt was the gay kid and the other boys made his life a misery, so he left school as soon as he could. The job in the poodle parlour didn't do him any favours really and the other kids used to pick on him something terrible. Sometimes Matt felt that life really wasn't worth living and there were moments when he even considered ending all. But Joanne once told him she couldn't possibly live without him and if he ended it then so would she. Bounder simply looked at him with those big brown eyes.

On the day he came out to his family, his mum simply cuddled him and said she always knew, but his dad had cooled a bit since he broke the news. Jesus, anyone would think it was catching. His younger brother was just a complete and utter arse and took every opportunity to get snide digs in about being 'queer'. Breaking the news of his sexual preference had changed the family dynamics and Matt became desperate to leave home.

As soon as he was eighteen, he applied to British Airways, mainly because he had heard that there was a high proportion of gay guys working as cabin crew. If only he could find someone like him, then maybe life wouldn't be so bad.

Matt loved every moment of his training. From the minute he walked through the door, everyone was friendly. They didn't ridicule him when he got something wrong and they laughed with him rather than at him. At long last he felt accepted. He had never felt that from anyone before, except for his mum and Joanne. Oh, and Bounder, of course.

CHAPTER 13

His training programme flew by and before he knew he was working on a real aircraft, with real colleagues and real passengers. Matt was in his element. Everyone liked Matt and he made friends easily. At long last, his true self was shining through, the chrysalis finally emerging as the butterfly.

He and a couple of colleagues eventually decided to share a flat close to the airport, so he packed up his stuff and left home. It upset his mum and she cried a lot. His dad seemed totally indifferent and as for his younger brother, well, the least said about him the better. He would miss Bounder, of course, but would visit as often as he could. He'd miss Joanne too, but she was away at university and completely besotted by a new boyfriend. Their lives were following different paths. It was time he led his own life anyway, and the continued love and support from Joanne had made it possible for him to at least try.

The flat share worked well. He and his flatmates mainly worked different shifts, so they rarely crowded the place. When they were all at home, they simply had a party.

Matt slogged his way up the ranks and promotion came his way. He was, however, waiting for that special day when he got the call to move to First Class. In the meantime, he simply carried on, loving what he was doing and loving who he was with. He had made friends around the world, some with benefits, some not, but he had not yet met that special person. There was still time. Never say never, Matt would always say.

So here he was, off to Rhodes for a few days with the gorgeous Demetrios. Matt and Demetrios worked together a few years back until Dem got homesick and applied for a job with Aegean Airlines so he could work out of Rhodes. Matt, who never liked to lose touch with friends because he had learnt to value them over the years, had kept in touch. They had formed a good friendship, so a few days spent with him was just what he needed.

And now he had met these two fun ladies on board the Rhodes flight and whilst they were past the first flush of youth, he would bet money on them being great fun on a night out. Oh yes, the week ahead was looking good, he thought, rubbing his hands together.

Chapter 14

Fiona and Donna made their way through the 'Nothing to Declare' section, with no problems. It had been a good flight and the pair had talked non-stop. Matt kept popping back to make sure they were OK, spending a few minutes with them whenever he could, and slipping them a few packets of pretzels.

All they had to do now was collect their luggage, find their holiday rep and get on the right coach to the hotel.

Most of the passengers were already on the coach by the time they bounced their hand luggage down the aisle, calling out cheery good mornings as they passed.

"Blimey, look at the glum faces on this lot. You'd think they were all going to a funeral instead of on holiday."

"Sssshhhh, Donna, they'll hear you," whispered Fiona, but she had to agree. They certainly were a miserable-looking bunch. Considering this was only day one, she wondered what on earth they would look like on the way home.

The final holidaymakers boarded the coach. A group of six, three men and three women, made their way towards the back. The smaller of the men looked at Donna and Fiona and winked as he made his way past. *Blimey*, Donna thought, *we've pulled again* as she turned to Fiona and imitated the man's wink.

"Don't worry, Fi," Donna smiled at her, "we can do much better than that."

After what seemed like a complete tour of the island dropping people off at various places, they finally pulled up outside their hotel. Winking Man and his friends, plus an elderly couple, were the only ones left on the bus.

Bloody hell, thought Donna, *I hope there's a bit more life in the hotel, otherwise we've made a crap choice.*

Two smiling girls waited for them behind the reception desk. Donna couldn't understand why they needed a desk that ran the entire length of the back wall for so few guests. A couple of people relaxed in the comfy looking chairs and sofas dotted here and there, but on the whole the place was very quiet. It didn't take long to check in and the pretty receptionist told them that their luggage would be delivered to their room shortly.

Donna gasped and, throwing the key cards onto the dressing table, opened the full-length glass door onto the balcony. The sun glinted off the turquoise blue water, and the golden sands of the not too crowded beach met her gaze. Their room was bright and cheerful, and the green cushions and runners on the beds eased the starkness of the white walls and light tiled floor. Fiona threw herself down on one of the beds and stretched out her arms and legs, totally happy to be there. She had forgotten all about Jeremy and was concentrating on having a wonderful time with her best friend, who she loved dearly and had missed so very much.

Unusual for hotels they found adequate hangers in the large wardrobe for all their clothes and after packing their stuff away, went off in search of food. Fiona felt her stomach rumble, they hadn't eaten since a very early breakfast, except for the odd packets of pretzels. Donna wasn't a fan of pretzels, she would have much preferred crisps, or even peanuts, but it was lovely of Matt to keep dropping them in her lap as he passed.

Wandering back downstairs, they found the outdoor terrace overlooking the large free-form swimming pool. The pool bar served food and drinks during the day but over half of the tables were empty. Fiona guessed that a lot of people were out on day trips, she hoped it would liven up later. Ordering a large Margherita pizza to share and a couple of beers, they settled for a relaxing afternoon. Liberal dollops of suncream and a quick change into shorts and tops had put them firmly in the holiday mood.

The afternoon flew and before they realised it was early evening. After a quick shower and another change of clothes, they made their way down to the bar; where else? Stretching along the entire wall, Donna was delighted to see the bar well stocked with a variety of bottles; in fact, everything a customer could ask for. Mirror tiles along the wall gave the illusion of space and depth, and far more bottles than there actually were. They chose a couple of stools right in the centre and, looking past their reflections in the tiles opposite, they had a clear view of what was going on behind. Picking up the cocktail menu, they chose mojitos for their first night, and agreed to make their way through the whole list by the end of the fortnight.

It was quiet in the bar. A few couples sat silently at tables for two. There was no conversation or laughter. The whole place lacked atmosphere.

"What the hell is wrong with these people?" asked Donna. "Surely if you go on holiday with someone the very least you could do was to talk to each other and try and enjoy yourself."

"That's a bit like me and Jeremy," said Fiona, "neither of us really have anything to say to each other. Jeremy talks at me rather than to me."

"Ah bless you, babe. Well that won't happen on this holiday because we will not stop talking."

There wasn't much change in the dining room; it was very subdued. Donna hoped it was because it was changeover day with guests going home and the new arrivals, knackered after a day of travelling, deciding on an early night. It was a good job Fiona had found a table next to the help-yourself wine bar. A couple of glasses later and they started to feel a little mellow, their laughter echoing around the room. It was clear to Donna that if they wanted any kind of fun in this place, it would have to be of their own making.

Doing a slow tour around the buffet area, Fiona was determined to engage her fellow guests in conversation. Some avoided her like the plague, happy to be in their own solitude, but others seemed quite happy to exchange pleasantries. Maybe she was imagining it, but there seemed to be a bit more of a buzz about the place as more people joined in.

Fiona couldn't decide what she wanted to eat and eventually the temptation to try a bit of everything won as she helped herself from the long rows of self-service cabinets. Hot and cold food was not only tempting to the eye, but the aromas soon had gastric juices flowing. Everything looked wonderful, colourful and appetizing. Both returned to their table with full plates and enjoyed their first delicious dinner, back in Rhodes after a very long time.

Much later and with full stomachs, they wandered out to the terrace bar where a music quiz was about to start. Fiona settled herself at a table and Donna headed off towards the bar. As she came back with two large glasses of white wine, she leaned over and whispered to Fiona.

"The Winking Man Gang are sitting right behind us. No, don't look round, Fi, it'll only encourage them."

"Good evening, girls, would you like to join us and make up a quiz team?"

"Fuck," muttered Donna under her breath. Winking Man was crouching down between them, his sweaty hand on her back made her skin crawl.

"We could do with a bit of glamour on our side, and we can't have you two beauties all on your own, can we?" he said with another wink. Or maybe he had a nasty tick. Whichever it was, it wasn't attractive. A small man with almost reptilian features, and a tongue that kept darting in and out of his mouth, there was something about him that Donna found quite repulsive.

The rest of the gang were already shuffling chairs around, making space, so they felt they didn't really have much choice other than being downright rude and pissing the gang off completely.

"So what do you two ladies do for work?" asked Winking Man's friend as they settled themselves into the chairs pulled up for them. He was much more presentable and had clearly made more of an effort with his appearance. His creased shirt at least looked clean, and he had slicked down his hair with water or some heavy-duty grease. The liberal dosing of cheap aftershave brought tears to Donna's eyes and she battled to control a coughing fit.

"I'm a bricklayer," said Fiona immediately.

"Blimey, what about your friend there?"

"She's a hod carrier."

"Oh, they don't look like they do those sorts of jobs, do they, Carol?" Carol shook her head, a vacant expression on her face. *Perhaps she was just tired after the journey*, Donna thought, giving her the benefit of the doubt.

"Do you work for a building company then?" asked Winking Man.

"No," replied Fiona, "we're both sub-contractors, so we pick up jobs as and when we want to. We've known each other for a long time and love being together. It all works fine."

Donna was looking more and more wide-eyed at Fiona's responses. Not only couldn't she believe what was coming out of her friend's mouth, but the change in her was staggering. She was almost back to the normal Fi that Donna loved.

Winking Man Gang were three couples, one of whom had recently married and were still all lovey-dovey. They seemed to keep themselves apart from the other two couples which was not totally surprising, and Donna wondered why they ever chose to be friends in the first place. Carol and the other woman, Gloria, were hard put to crack a smile between them, sporting faces like a couple of slapped arses. Donna couldn't imagine a worse group of friends to be with on a night out. But hey, it was only the first night and they would make sure not to be caught by them again.

The evening wore on and the wine flowed. The music was loud and Donna couldn't hear a word Fiona said, so she started texting. It wasn't long before the pair were rolling around with laughter and tears poured down their faces at the ridiculous comments they were each making. Winking Man and his mate clearly wanted to join in, but thankfully they were wise enough to heed the evil eye directed at them from the sour faced Carol and the equally dour Gloria.

They didn't win the music quiz. The gang was hopeless and didn't take any notice of Fiona or Donna, who had spent a lot of their youth in various dens of iniquity around the world, and had a good grasp on the music scene. The girls eventually made their excuses, claiming tiredness after the early start and travelling and said their goodnights.

"Phew, what a first day, eh?" said Donna as they prepared for bed.

"Do you know what, Don, I've had the best time ever! The funniest was when you went off to the loo and then came back ten minutes later and asked 'where was I going?' and went off again. I mean, where the bloody hell had you been for ten minutes?"

Donna started laughing, "Well, I saw the sign for the toilet pointing down the stairs but when I got to the bottom there were no more signs. There was no one around to ask so I opened a door but ended up in some sort of stationery cupboard. I got a bit side-tracked; you know what I'm like with notepads and pens and stuff ever since we saw that documentary about HM Stationery Office. Anyway, I had a bit of a browse, then thought I shouldn't really be in here but it took me a while to find the door. By the time I got out I

CHAPTER 14

forgot where I was going in the first place so thought I'd just come back to you and start again."

"You left me with Winking Man who kept asking what was taking you so long."

"What did you tell him?"

"I told him you had a problem with wind and that shut him up. They probably won't ask us to sit with them again."

They both fell into bed, laughing. *And this was only day one,* thought Fiona as she drifted off to sleep.

Chapter 15

Thursday

Up bright and early the next morning and raring to go, which was a bit of a miracle considering how much alcohol they had consumed the night before, they enjoyed a full English for breakfast before making their way into the Old Town.

The sun sparkled like small gemstones on the ocean and the cooling breeze lifted their hair as they followed the other tourists. The twenty-minute walk took them in the right direction, although Fiona wondered at one point whether they might have to make an emergency stop for the loo. Donna had always suffered with her stomach for as long as she had known her, but this morning, it seemed particularly bad. Probably due to the change of water and different food, she reasoned. She could never understand how so much noise could come out of one small arse.

"Donna, can't you control that?"

"Er, no I can't. Anyway, it's better out than in."

"Do you know if we were ever attacked I could shove you under my arm, point your arse at the enemy and use you as a Gatling gun!" Fiona remarked, and the pair of them laughed their way into town. The more Donna laughed, the more uncontrollable her wind became, and the more she farted the more she laughed.

The Old Town didn't disappoint at all. As they entered through one of the ten gates within the walls of the medieval city it was like being transported back in time and the distinct change of atmosphere was palpable. Cobbled streets and old buildings gave a strong sense of those who lived centuries ago and, whilst neither of them was very much into history, they couldn't help but feel the drama of the place. Over two hundred narrow streets and alleys, many with no names, were crowded with shops and tavernas tempting browsing tourists inside.

The first stop was coffee and a much-needed toilet break. They found a table at a corner café and settled themselves for an hour of people watching. Fiona ordered a couple of cappuccinos whilst Donna went off in search of the loo.

"The loo's not bad," she said when she returned. "It's fairly clean, flushes and has toilet paper, it's dark in there though." They always used to take it in turns to suss out the toilets wherever they went. Their needs were simple, toilet paper and a loo that flushed, rather than chuck it in a bucket like many of the toilets across Greece. The older they became the more they wanted their creature comforts, like proper sanitation. If toilets were bad, then the one who didn't do the check would wait until the next place.

After coffee they headed for the shops, stopping often to buy little trinkets that caught their eye. Owners standing outside the jewellery shops enticed them in, and they both bought some beautiful turquoise earrings and necklaces as birthday gifts to themselves, the colour forever reminding them of the turquoise waters of Rhodes.

The Old Town was packed with tourists jostling for space in the small shops, and it seemed to be getting hotter by the second.

"Shall we stop in that taverna and have a beer?" suggested Fiona as she headed off to grab the table that a couple had just left. Sinking gratefully into chairs they popped their purchases underneath. Donna picked up the menu card wedged between the oil and vinegar bottles in the middle of the table. It was getting busy as the lunchtime crowds made their way in. Ordering a large beer and a Greek salad each, they settled back to some more people watching and talked about their plans for the rest of their holiday.

They agreed to pop into a little tourist place they had passed near their hotel and book a day-trip to Symi for the following day. They discussed the merits of hiring a car and touring around the island. Donna said she was happy to drive and had her driving licence with her, but Fiona was reluctant. She eventually agreed that it would be the best way to see Rhodes, so yes, as long as Donna did the driving. Not that Fiona didn't like driving, but driving at home was different. She knew the area and what lane she needed to be in. She was much less confident when she didn't know where she was going, let alone driving on the wrong side of the road.

It was moments like these that Fiona missed Jeremy taking control. *No,* she thought as she shook herself, *I've got to forget Jeremy because for the next couple of weeks he simply does not exist.*

The waiter brought their salads and placing them on the table, he leant down on both elbows and gazed at Donna.

"Would you like to meet with me in Falaraki this evening, beautiful lady?"

"Er, why?"

"We could enjoy the nightlife or simply think of other ways to entertain ourselves, yes?"

"Umm, sorry but no," Donna said as she picked up Fiona's hand. "As you can see, I'm already spoken for."

"Ahhh." The waiter gave a knowing smile and moved away to take the orders from another table which two younger girls had just claimed.

"What was that all about?" laughed Fiona.

"Much better a little white lie than to hurt his feelings. Anyway, I am spoken for, I have you and I would never leave you on your own. I've got Dave too, plus we're off out with Matt tonight, if you remember."

The salads looked delicious; tomatoes, cucumber, onions and olives made a colourful combination and the slab of feta cheese on top drizzled with olive oil and sprinkled with oregano added the finishing touch. Donna couldn't resist dipping the bread into the bottom of her bowl, soaking up the oil and crumbly bits of cheese. She just about emptied the bread basket.

After lunch they took a slow walk back to the hotel. Matt phoned to say he would be with them by seven and did they mind if he brought Demetrios with him? He told them not to eat dinner because he had an idea if they were up for it.

If they were up for it indeed! They were back on holiday together, so why on earth would they not be up for it.

CHAPTER 16

Matt and Demetrios arrived on time and, as expected, found Donna and Fiona in the bar, sipping cocktails. Introductions made, more drinks ordered, the four of them wandered outside to the quieter terrace at the front of the hotel, overlooking the beach and calm waters beyond. They talked about themselves a bit, getting to know one another. Matt and Demetrios met when they both worked for the same airline in the UK, but Demetrios told the girls that he missed his family far too much and wanted to move back home. Although both he and Matt had a bit of a fling a few years back, they now remained just good friends, sometimes with benefits. Demetrios was totally up front about his life, and it was refreshing to hear such honesty.

Demetrios was gorgeous. Dark hair, brown eyes, olive skin, a full sensuous mouth with the whitest teeth ever, and a body that he clearly looked after. Not only did he look good, but he also smelt amazing and for a moment Donna was transfixed by his bronzed neck peering over the white collar of his shirt. She could just imagine nuzzling up close, soaking up his smell. She shook her head quickly, bringing herself back to the moment. Demetrios was nice and friendly, easy to talk to and flashed his beautiful teeth in a constantly smiley face, which totally mesmerised Fiona. There was nothing not to like about Demetrios.

"So, what's the plan for this evening, Matt?" Fiona was nearing the end of her cocktail and didn't want to order another if they were soon to move on.

"Well, we wondered if you two would be up for a comedy drag club. There's this new place that's just opened in town and it's had some excellent reviews. It also serves food so we can eat, drink and watch the show. What do you reckon?"

"Oh yeah, I'm totally up for that. Fi?"

"Absolutely! Are we off now or have we got time for another drink?"

"We've got time for another drink before we need to leave."

"Great, Fi and I will go and get them and then we won't have to pay. Same again?"

Matt and Demetrios nodded and the girls made their way to the bar.

"What do you think, Fi? Aren't they both gorgeous?"

"Yes, they are," replied Fiona. "I can't stop looking at Demetrios' teeth, I find his mouth quite hypnotic when he speaks. Yeah, I think we're going to have a great evening with them."

"Ladies," Matt said when they got back to the table with the drinks, "what would you think to a day out with us both? Demetrios would love to show you the Valley of the Butterflies. It won't take all day, but we could go on and do a tour of the island. But only if you want to."

"Matt, Demetrios, that would be lovely and yes, we'd love to come, wouldn't we, Fi?"

"Yes, it sounds fascinating. Does it really have butterflies or is that just the name given to it?"

"No, it has butterflies," replied Demetrios. "Hundreds and thousands of them. It's a nature reserve and a beautiful walk through the valley. It's full of trees, ponds, waterfalls, bridges and it's such a lovely natural environment. Apparently, the butterflies go there to complete the final stages of their life cycle and every inch of the trees and logs are taken by sleeping butterflies. But if you whistle or clap your hands it wakes them up and they fly. Thousands of butterflies flying through the valley. It is a truly magical sight."

Matt had been to the valley several times and never got tired of its magical energies. He would love to go again, and it was just the place he wanted to show the girls.

"Wow," exclaimed Donna. "Yes, I would absolutely love to go. We're off to Symi for the day tomorrow and were then planning a relaxing day by the pool the day after, so could we go the day after that? Does that fit into your flying schedules?"

"Yes, fine with me. Is that OK with you, Dem?" Demetrios nodded.

"That's settled then. We can arrange times later, but now I think we had better get going if we want to get a table."

The club was already heaving with holidaymakers when they arrived, but they were shown to a table with an excellent view of the stage and handed menus. The food wasn't fancy by any means. Everything seemed to come in a basket, but they each found something they liked and placed their order, plus a round of drinks.

The show was hilarious. The sound of laughter filled the room, the audience holding their stomachs, wiping away tears as they rolled down cheeks, finding it hard to catch their breath. Donna felt sure she had just peed herself a little. The stage lights glinted off the colourful sequined costumes of the drag artists, which were worthy of a glitzy Las Vegas show. Not only did those guys do side-splitting comedy, they sang too and soon had everyone clapping and singing along. The curtains closed, then one by one the artists came back on stage, minus make-up and outfits and it was an eye-opener to see the ordinary looking men behind the glitz. A few final songs, and that was it. Show over.

What a bloody shame, thought Fiona – it was an evening she never wanted to end.

As they waited for a taxi to take them back to their hotel, Donna reminded Matt that they were off to Symi the following day but would message when they got back. Hopefully there would also be time for a couple of drinks as well as the Butterfly Valley before he had to fly back to the UK. They hugged and kissed goodnight, and the two couples went their separate ways.

"What an amazing first day," said Fiona in the taxi on the way back to the hotel. "I have to say that I think you were right about Matt. He is simply gorgeous, there's nothing not to like, is there? Demetrios is fabulous too."

"Yeah, they're both great and wonderful company for a night out. I really enjoyed this evening, Fi, what a brilliant start to the holiday, eh?"

"You know, Donna, I'm so happy you suggested it, and I'm even happier that I told Jeremy that it was not up for negotiation. Perhaps I should be just a little more assertive when I get back home."

"Mmm," murmured Donna, "I think that's the best idea you've had all day."

Chapter 17

Friday

Their trip to Symi started early the next morning, so after a quick breakfast of toast and marmalade they had very little time to get down to the boat. They made it with just a few minutes to spare and climbed to the upper deck. Squeezing between two families towards the front of the boat and with a fair bit of wriggling about, they claimed the space they needed. Feeling a little hungover from the night before, Donna hoped that the almost two-hour crossing would be a smooth one.

The sea air was bracing and revitalising and it wasn't too long before their laughter was ringing out across the Aegean Sea. They soon attracted attention and within minutes the security guy appeared.

"Bloody hell," said Donna, nudging Fiona in the ribs. "Just look at that!"

They both looked over and their jaws dropped. Security was indeed a reason to get arrested. Tall and dark, his tight-fitting black uniform adorned with gold badges showed off his muscular body to perfection. A peak cap, Ray-Ban Aviators and some sort of weapon at the hip completed the look. He stood with arms folded and legs apart, looking all mean and moody and it took them a full minute to realise they were staring open-mouthed and the rest of the female passengers were following their gaze. Even the toothless little old Greek lady, who must have been well into her nineties, was staring with a faraway look on her face, obviously remembering days gone by. Security had clearly achieved the result he wanted and moved on.

Their first stop on the trip was Archangel Michael's Monastery to the south of the island. As they rounded the promontory and sailed into the small harbour, the view was stunning. The sun glinted off the white and lemon buildings, the ornate bell tower taking centre stage against the backdrop of the rugged hills. It was a stunning scene, the light perfectly illuminating the small town. Donna could imagine coming here as an artist and spending her days on the quayside with a brush and canvas, although she had never painted in her life. The boat's tannoy system crackled to life as the captain announced they had just over an hour before setting off for the north of the island and the main town and port on Symi.

Fiona and Donna made their way off the boat and headed straight for the Monastery of Archangel Michael, which they were both keen to see. Everyone seemed to have the same idea, and they joined the back of the queue. They were not disappointed. The monastery was rebuilt in 1783 but dated back to the 6th century. Dedicated to Archangel Michael, the church was adorned with beautiful frescoes and icons and conveyed serenity and calmness, and in true tradition they lit a candle before leaving. A look around the monastery preceded the obligatory gift shop where they each bought a few souvenirs.

It was time to head back to the boat for the next part of the trip.

"I just need a wee first, Donna. Can you hold these while I pop in?" Fiona passed her bags over to Donna and headed into the toilet. The longer Donna stood outside waiting the more she needed to go herself and as soon as Fiona reappeared, they swapped places.

"Got to go," she said, handing everything over to Fiona and rushed into the toilet. It took Donna an age. *What an earth is*

CHAPTER 17

she doing in there? wondered Fiona, getting more and more fidgety. Finally, the door opened.

"Sorry, Fi," she said when she emerged ten minutes later, "but my bowel's erupting again and I didn't want to risk getting back on the boat. So sorry."

"Well, you can't help it, but we'd better get a move on cos we're cutting it fine now."

They made their way down to the harbour as fast as their flipflops would allow.

"Fuck fuck fuckety fuck," exclaimed Donna, pointing to the back end of the boat as it made its way out through the harbour walls.

Chapter 18

"Shit, Donna, what the hell do we do now?"

"I don't know."

"I wonder if there's anyone around this place who's going to the port and could give us a lift. If we can get there, we can still catch the boat back to Rhodes." Fiona felt it might be a bit too optimistic. The monastery had a deserted feel about it. Everyone had left.

"We could get on the next boat that comes in," suggested Donna.

"We could, but the problem with that is we have no idea when the next boat is due or where it's going. We could end up in Timbuk-bloody-tu!!"

"What do you suggest?"

"Let's see if we can find someone," suggested Fiona, "we can't stand here all day debating what we should do next, we have to be active."

There was not a soul to be seen as they wandered around the monastery. They headed back into the gift shop, nobody there either. With the departure of the boatful of tourists, everyone had scuttled away to get on with their daily tasks until the next boat came in. Fiona and Donna were getting more and more desperate and had visions of spending the night in a place that seemed to have had the life sucked out of it. It was not a welcoming thought.

A faint sound of whistling carried on the breeze. Fiona and Donna stood still looking at each other and, as if with one mind, turned and rushed towards the sound.

They found the source at the back of the gift shop.

"*Kalemera*," called Donna. The man looked up, clearly surprised to see them.

"*Kalemera*," he replied.

"Do you speak English?" she asked, pronouncing each syllable in the same loud tone, as if speaking to an idiot.

"*Oxi*." The women looked at each other and shrugged. The limit of Donna's Greek extended to good morning, good evening, thank you and a large white wine please.

The man went back to loading boxes into the back of a white pickup truck that looked a little the worse for wear. Donna tried again with her loud, monosyllabic approach.

"We need to go to port – you take us?" Gesticulating wildly and pointing in a direction that she hoped conveyed distance, she looked like a possessed dervish.

Clearly understanding English better than he could speak it, he nodded his head vigorously and held up ten fingers. They hoped that meant in ten minutes they would be on their way to the port and safely onto the boat heading back to Rhodes.

Both Donna and Fiona smiled, nodded manically and gave the thumbs-up sign.

"Donna," she said, patting her chest, "Fiona," patting Fi's chest before Fi started swatting her hand away. "You?" Donna questioned.

"Ahh," he said, patting his own chest vigorously. "Costas."

Introductions made, the girls were eager to set off, but Costas appeared to be in no hurry. A Greek ten minutes was nothing like a British ten minutes. Costas continued loading boxes into the truck. A large man with an enormous belly overhanging his trousers, he obviously found the manual labour hard work as sweat poured from his brow. A fringe of what was once dark hair but now peppered with shades of grey showed around the back and sides of his head, and the grey stubble belied a lack of shaving rather than any cultivated designer look. Nevertheless, Costas had a kind, smiling face, and his blue eyes twinkled under the brim of his cloth cap.

The entire island was only about ten miles from top to bottom so it shouldn't take them long to reach the town where their boat would be docking any minute now. But they had no idea what the roads were like, and if Costas didn't get a move on, they feared they would never get there.

As he loaded in the last box he indicated they should get into the truck. Donna swept the empty food packets and chocolate wrappings to the floor to join the ever growing heap as she climbed onto the bench seat. Cigarette packets lined the dashboard, and rosary beads hung from the rear-view mirror. Considering this was a working vehicle, Costas took little pride in it.

Costas huffed and puffed and heaved his bulk behind the steering wheel and started the engine. Mopping his brow with a greying, fetid rag that may once have been a white handkerchief, it was clear the heat was getting to him. With no air conditioning in the truck, he wound down his window and indicated that Fiona should do the same.

"Eeet no long before port," he said, turning on the radio and blasting out the dulcet tones of Demis Roussos.

The cooling breeze through the windows with the pungent scent of wild herbs was wonderful, and the girls relaxed as visions of their boat drew ever closer. The drive along the narrow bumpy roads was pleasant enough, and the rugged scenery was in sheer contrast to the green fields they were used to back at home. Costas' driving left a lot to be desired and the truck started to weave from side to side and gather speed. Donna looked across at him in alarm as she and Fiona grabbed at anything to keep themselves secure in their seats. She didn't think Costas looked very well at all. The colour had drained from his face, he looked grey and still the sweat ran in rivulets down his cheeks.

"Costas, are you OK? Can you slow down a bit, please?"

There was no answer, and suddenly the trucked skewed off to the right and ploughed through the rough bushes, bouncing over rocks. The girls hung on for dear life, Donna calling and shaking Costas to get a response.

Slowly the truck came to a stop as it scraped along a boulder. It was a miracle that it remained on four wheels. All was silent for what seemed like an age then, as if in slow motion, Costas slumped forward over the steering wheel, his face pressing against the horn, which was deafening in the silence of their stillness.

"What the bloody hell just happened?" asked Donna, clearly shaken.

"I don't think Costas is very well." Fiona was looking across at the man slumped over in the driving seat.

"Not very well is a bit of an understatement, Fi," replied Donna, as she moved her hand away from Costas' neck.

"He's dead."

Chapter 19

"What do you mean he's dead? He can't be dead. He can't die on us now, we're not back at the port yet. Donna, do something, you're the nurse." Fiona was becoming a touch hysterical and climbed out of the pickup.

"Calm down, Fiona. I can't do anything."

"You must be able to do something, you can't let him die."

"Fiona, I can't do anything – watch my mouth, he is dead."

"Well, give him mouth to mouth, there's got to be something you can do."

"Fiona, he's dead. I am not Jesus and this is not Lazarus. I cannot bring him back to life. He is dead, gone, kaput, no longer, deceased!" she said as she ran the side of her hand across her throat.

Donna gently eased Costas' body away from the steering wheel, the silence audible.

"What do we do now?" asked Fiona, as she calmed down a little, trying to process the fact that Costas was indeed dead.

"The only thing we can do," replied Donna, "is to drive ourselves to the port and hand Costas over to the authorities."

"I'm not going all the way to the port sitting next to a dead body. Can we put him in the back?"

"Seriously? Have you seen the size of him?"

"We can do it, you pull and I'll push," said Fiona climbing back into the truck and pushing Costas out of the driver's side door.

It took a while, but eventually they got the top half of his body manoeuvred around so they could slide him out of the vehicle. Donna kept apologising to him for the indignities they were putting him through. She had been a nurse long enough, and present at many deaths, to believe that the soul went onwards to a better place and she had visions of Costas looking down on them and not being too overjoyed with what they were doing with his body.

Dragging him round to the back of the truck, Donna let the tailgate down and they shoved and heaved and finally got him into the back amongst the white boxes. With the heat and all the exertion they sat panting on the ground, totally exhausted. Donna's hair was plastered to her head and Fiona's once immaculate white T-shirt was smeared with dirt and had big damp patches under the arms.

"Right, let's get going," said Fiona as she got to her feet. "You drive and I'll navigate."

"Oh blimey," exclaimed Donna, as she slid behind the steering wheel. "I've never driven one of these things with the gear stick up here." She fiddled about and quickly discovered that the column gear stick easily slotted into different gears, although she had no idea whether she was in first, second or third. Considering the age of the truck she doubted that there were any gears beyond that except reverse. But this was going to be trial and error all the way to the port, so they might as well just get going and see what happened.

Donna selected a gear and slowly pressed down on the accelerator and eased off the clutch. They shot forward with a lurch, she slammed on the brake. She selected another slot

CHAPTER 19

for the gear stick and bingo, the truck moved backwards. She reversed slowly and got back onto the road, selected another gear and, with much revving of the engine, they shot forward.

Fiona was fiddling with Google Maps on her phone and prayed she had enough battery and the signal remained strong. She hit 'get directions' and a map of the area appeared.

"OK, so basically you just keep going straight and we'll get there eventually," she said, "but there are a lot of bendy bits which might be tricky." *Brilliant instructions*, thought Donna, as she finally found what she thought was top gear and the engine stopped revving so hard.

The road wasn't too bad, bumpy and rough in places, but then Donna was used to that with all the potholes on the roads at home. She didn't want to push the truck too hard, and she was still getting to grips with the gear stick, but she was beginning to think that Costas' 'eeet no long before port' was more wishful thinking than fact.

Glimpses of the sun glistening on the water in the distance gave them hope and, still heading straight, they saw the town start to take shape as they finally drove down to the harbour. Fiona tapped 'police station' into her phone and told Donna to turn left at the end of the road, then just follow the harbour.

They were never more relieved than when they saw the sign on the front of the large white building. Although mainly in Greek, the word 'police' at the bottom was clear enough and Donna brought the truck to a stop and switched off the engine.

"Right, Fi, you go in and get somebody and I'll stay here with Costas."

Fiona got out and made her way up the steps and into the building. Approaching a man in uniform behind the desk, she prayed he could speak English. She had no idea how to make him understand that she had a dead body in the back of the truck if he couldn't.

"Excuse me, but do you speak English?"

"Yes."

"Well then, erm, my friend and I have, erm, come from Archangel Michael's Monastery and the man who was giving us a lift has, erm, died and we had to drive his truck here."

"Yes."

"Well the man, Costas, is in the back of the truck."

"Yes."

"Well, he's dead."

"Dead?"

"Yes dead! Can you come and deal with it please, because we have to catch the boat back to Rhodes soon?"

The police officer strode out of the building, Fiona running behind him.

"Where truck?"

"There." Fiona pointed to where Donna had haphazardly parked it and was standing by the tailgate keeping watch over Costas.

"It's OK now, Costas, the police officer is coming, and we've got help for you," she whispered.

The police officer walked over to where Donna was standing and peered into the back of the pickup at the body of Costas nestled between the boxes. He made the sign of a cross across his upper body and whilst muttering something in Greek, grabbed his radio and sent off some rapid instructions to his colleague inside the building.

Within seconds the door to the police station burst open and a couple of young officers ran down the steps and

CHAPTER 19

across to the truck. They too performed the crossing and muttering ritual when they saw Costas' body lying in the back of the truck. Officer number one issued instructions, the pair jumped into the truck and drove it off around the side of the police station.

"You two, come."

All Donna and Fiona wanted to do was find their boat back to Rhodes, but Fiona guessed the police officer needed to take their statements to establish what had happened. He led them inside the building and into a spartan interview room, with whitewashed walls and beige tiled floor

"You sit, I come back," he said pointing to a table and four chairs in the middle of the room.

"I hope he gets a shift on and doesn't work in Greek time," said Donna pulling out one of the chairs. "I want to get out of here and back to Rhodes." She was feeling the strain of it all. Her limbs ached with pulling and pushing Costas. She was sweaty, dirty and tired. All she wanted was a hot shower, a change of clothes and a long, cold beer.

Ten minutes later, and Officer One was back with paper and pen in hand.

"OK, you tell me what happened."

Fiona explained the sequence of events since their arrival in Symi as best she could, although she left out Donna's bowels. Donna filled in with some of the missing bits and pieces as Officer One scribbled away on his pad.

"OK, stay here." He left the room. The pair were becoming more and more agitated and eager to leave. They couldn't afford to miss the boat, they didn't relish the thought of being stranded on the island. They had told him everything that happened, so there was no reason for them to stay any longer. After all, if he needed them, he could always find them at their hotel in Rhodes.

Twenty minutes later and he was back, this time with Officers Two and Three behind him.

"I will now detain you on suspicion of murder and drug smuggling." He moved aside as the two officers took hold of Donna and Fiona by the arms and started moving them towards the door.

"No, no," shouted Donna, "you've got this all wrong. He's had a heart attack; we didn't murder him! Why would we do that? There are no drugs either, he's got ornaments from the gift shop. No, you can't do this. We're innocent. We need to catch the boat back to Rhodes." But all of Donna's shouting and pleading had no effect as the officers led them away to the cells.

Chapter 20

"What the fuck do we do now?" asked Donna, standing in the middle of the cell looking at the whitewashed walls and tiled floor, and grimacing as she saw the stainless-steel bucket in the corner, with a toilet roll on the floor next to it. The whole place stank of excrement and stale bodies.

"I don't know," said Fiona sitting on one of the single beds pushed against the wall. "They've got our bags with our phones and nobody knows we're here. We have no choice but to wait and see what happens next."

Donna sat down on the other bed and faced Fiona, each were lost in their own thoughts. Eventually Fiona looked up.

"Right, thinking about this logically now. They will have to do a post-mortem on Costas and then they'll discover he died of natural causes so they can't charge us with murder. I have no idea where the drugs came from, they're obviously inside those boxes but they will not find our fingerprints anywhere near them so they have no evidence to charge us with involvement there. They will have to let us go."

"Except that my fingerprints will be on some boxes because I shifted them around to make space to get Costas in the back."

"Fuck!" replied Fiona, as her head sunk downwards again.

"What's that noise?" asked Fiona, a short time later. "Someone's coming."

"No, it's coming from outside," Donna replied, pointing up towards the narrow window between the two beds.

They could hear voices and other sounds coming from what they presumed to be the back of the building.

"Let's pull one of these beds across and see if I can climb up on the frame and see what's going on." They pulled the bed over. Fiona shuddered to think what the stains on the grimy mattress might be as Donna clambered onto it, grabbed hold of the window bars and pulled herself up onto the frame.

"Bugger, I can't see out. I'm too short, Fi, you try."

They swapped places and Fiona got eye-level with the window.

"I can see Officer One and another man standing by the truck. There's a dark red van parked alongside, and the man is talking to Officer One. Costas has gone. Hang on, the second man is opening the van. Officer One is taking the boxes out of the truck and putting them in the van. They're both doing it now."

"That all seems a bit shifty. Why would they move the boxes of ornaments?" asked Donna.

"Unless they're not ornaments at all, perhaps that's where the drugs are that he keeps on about."

"What's the other man look like?" Donna hoped they wouldn't need a good description and this was all a bit of a misunderstanding, but best to be prepared. The chances of them catching the boat back to Rhodes that day were fading by the minute.

"Oh, he's horrible. He's looks shifty. He keeps glancing around like he's worried someone might see him. I don't like the look of him at all, I wouldn't trust him an inch."

CHAPTER 20

"Yeah, but really look at him, Fi, can you see any marks or tattoos that you would recognise again?"

"He's got a scar down his left cheek. It's hard to see how big but it starts at the corner of his eye and then goes down into his stubble. He's got dark curly hair, probably brown eyes, but I can't see them and he's quite swarthy. I don't like him; he looks a real slimeball."

"That's great, anything else?"

"They've finished putting the boxes in the van. The truck is empty now. They're talking, waving their arms about. It all sounds quite panicky, but I can't understand the words. Slimeball is getting in the van. He's moving, yep he's driving off. Officer One is coming back into the building. Shit! He's just looked up and seen me watching!! Fucking hell, Donna, he's seen me!!"

"OK," said Donna, trying to remain calm but feeling her friend's fear, "don't panic, we're going to get out of this mess, I promise you. I don't know how yet, but we will get out."

Fiona got off the bed and they quickly moved it back to where it should be. They sat down opposite one another again.

"They've probably got some sort of drug ring going, and Officer One is in it right up to his dirty little neck. I'm sure he'll try to implicate us somehow just to save his own arse. Well, we can't do anything more right now, we'll just have to wait for his next move." Donna sounded a lot braver than she felt.

CHAPTER 21

Officer One broke out in a cold sweat. *Skata!* One of the English women had seen him moving the boxes into the van, which could possibly implicate him.

Yiorgos Kallis had a lucrative little side-line going with the Albanians for almost three years now and he wasn't keen to give it up. It started with a chance meeting with a big Albanian guy down by the port. The Albanian offered him several packs of cannabis to turn a blind eye to a passport infringement. Kallis accepted, split the pack and, keeping some for himself, sold the rest.

He soon started supplying the locals with the odd pack here and there, and before he knew it demand outstripped supply. He ordered more and more from the Albanians and, as time went by, the drugs grew harder and his network of customers grew bigger. Eventually Kallis found the means to distribute further afield and took on more of the smaller Greek islands. He was now their chief supplier. The Albanians dropped off the goods at the monastery, Tobias repackaged it into smaller quantities and Costas drove them to the port for distribution. The perfect set-up. He didn't even have to get his hands dirty.

Kallis was full of his own self-importance. In his late twenties, he had the swagger of a cocky little shit. He wasn't popular, but he didn't care. In his own little mind he was living the life of a major drug baron, and the fact that he was a police officer kept him above suspicion and above the law. He got what he wanted by instilling fear and even his own colleagues at the police station were a little scared of him, secretly hoping that one day he would get his comeuppance. Kallis was a big fish in a little pond.

But today Costas had totally pissed him off. What as the idiot thinking, offering to drive the two English women to the port when he had boxes of drugs in the back of the truck? And why on earth did he have to die at the same time? Totally inconsiderate.

And now there was a fly in the ointment and he needed to get it out. If only those two women had just minded their own business, he would have let them go, eventually. But no, one of them had to peer out of the window and she had seen him. She had seen Tobias too, and he wouldn't trust him not to talk. He really needed to come up with some sort of plan that would keep them quiet.

He phoned Tobias at the monastery and, after a twenty-minute call, the pair had come up with a plan. Well, to be honest, it was Kallis who came up with the plan, and Tobias just listened. Tobias was incapable of coming up with any sort of plan to save his life.

Tobias would explain the situation to the Albanians and ask them to collect the English women from the main port after dark that night. Kallis would collect the women from the cell and walk them round to the port and hand them over. What the Albanians did with them after that was no concern of his, but at least they would be off his island and all would be well in his world again.

Kallis ended the call, feeling happier that he had come up with an arrangement that would not only safeguard him, but the entire operation. He just needed to get the women out of the cells with no questions being asked. He would deal with the paperwork later.

Twenty minutes later his phone rang and Tobias' name flashed up on the screen.

CHAPTER 21

"They won't come tonight," Tobias said. "Too busy with another job, but can come tomorrow."

Kallis was fuming. What was wrong with Tobias, why couldn't he do one simple thing?

"Fine," he shouted down the phone, "but you make sure it happens tomorrow or we're all in big trouble."

Chapter 22

Saturday

Matt hit the end call button and threw his phone onto the sofa.

"What's wrong?" asked Demetrios.

"I'm concerned about Donna and Fiona. I've been calling both their phones since yesterday afternoon and all I get is voicemail. Surely one of them would have picked up." Matt was starting to seriously worry. He had not spoken to the girls since their night out and he felt sure they would have at least answered him.

"Well, you've only just met them and you don't really know them at all. Perhaps this is normal for them. Perhaps they didn't like you as much as you thought they did."

"Mmm, maybe. But Donna did say she would message when they got back from Symi. I'm not getting a good feeling about this. I might just pop round to their hotel, just to make sure they're OK. It will put my mind at rest if nothing else."

"Do you want me to come with you?"

"No, no, Demetrios, that's fine. I shouldn't be too long then we can go out somewhere for lunch."

"You will probably find them lying in the sun by the pool. They said they were going to have a relaxing day after their trip to Symi."

"I hope so," said Matt, as he grabbed his keys and phone and set off.

The hotel wasn't too far and the twenty-minute walk would do him good. It was a typical Greek morning, beautiful clear blue skies and the sun glinting off the sea, the warm air hinting of the heat that was still to come.

"*Kalemera*," said Matt, approaching the attractive young woman behind the reception desk. "I'm looking for my friends, Fiona and Donna, the two English women who arrived last week. I'm just wondering if they're here at the moment."

"One moment, please," she said turning to her screen on the front desk and tapping on the keyboard. "Do you have surnames, please?"

"Oh, I'm not sure. One is Chambers, I think, but I can't remember the other one."

"One moment," she said as she typed something. "Ah yes, here we are. They should still be here, no checking out yet."

"Yes, I know they're not due to check out for another week or so, but are they here at this moment?"

"I call their room." She pressed a few buttons on the phone, but Matt could hear it ringing and ringing. "There is no answer, maybe they gone out."

Matt was not convinced, but clearly he was not going to get much further here. Unsure what to do next, he slowly turned away from the desk.

"Wait." The receptionist beckoned him back. "Maybe I should not be telling you this, but there is a note attached to their room from housekeeping. It seems your friends have not been back for the last twenty-four hours, they did not use their room last night."

CHAPTER 22

"Thank you, yes that's very helpful. They went on a trip to Symi on Friday morning and I haven't heard from them since."

"It's looking like they not come back from there."

Matt didn't know whether to be pleased or not. At least the girls were not ignoring him, especially after their fabulous night out together. But on the other hand, if they had not returned from Symi, then something must be wrong.

Keeping up a brisk pace he walked back to the apartment, mulling over all the reasons why they had not returned. None of them were positive. He couldn't think of one good reason why they hadn't returned to Rhodes or why they wouldn't have answered their phones.

"Demetrios," he shouted as he rushed through the door of the apartment. "They've gone, something's wrong, they've not come back from Symi. What do we do?"

"Calm down. There's got to be a logical reason why they've not come back. Maybe they missed the boat and had to stay overnight?"

"No, they would have answered their phones if that were the case." Matt started pacing around the open-plan space of the kitchen and living area. It wasn't a small area by any means, but he covered it in record time. He was clearly worried.

"Yes, but what if their phones had died, or they can't get a signal? Let's phone around some hotels near the harbour – you do some and I'll do some, OK?"

"OK." Matt got a pen and some paper and started googling hotels on Symi. He soon had a list of telephone numbers and he and Demetrios began phoning around.

Half an hour later and they'd had no joy. None of the places they called had two English women checking in.

"What if they've had an accident?" said Matt.

"Let's check with the local medical centre. I know there's one near the port so we'll start there."

Fifteen minutes later and again, nothing. There had been no casualties or reports of accidents on the island within the last twenty-four hours.

"Right, I'm going to the police." Matt felt it was his only option. He couldn't shake off the feeling that something was seriously wrong.

"Let's go to the local police here. I have a friend, a detective, who might help. He can certainly talk to the Symi police."

Matt and Demetrios headed for the police station. Matt prayed that Demetrios' friend would be there and willing to help. They were in luck. Yiannis Doukas was delighted to see his friend and only too happy to help if he could. He ushered them into a side room and listened patiently to their story. Although he didn't think there was a real problem, he agreed to check with the police on Symi as a favour to Demetrios, who he secretly had a bit of a crush on. He left the room with promises that he would be back as soon as he had some information.

The wait seemed to go on forever. Matt was getting more fidgety and began pacing the room.

"Sit down, Matt. At least something is happening now and Yiannis will be back soon with some good news, I'm sure."

Yiannis returned with a colleague and they took seats on the opposite side of the table. Matt knew that this would not be the news he'd hoped for.

"This is my boss, Lieutenant Christos Iraklidis," said Yiannis, "Senior Investigating Officer within the Detective Division. We have a little information." Yiannis Doukas was a Sergeant Investigating Officer within the same division and he figured a quick phone call to Symi police might just put everyone's mind at rest. Surprised by the response, Yiannis knew he had no choice but to involve his boss.

CHAPTER 22

"OK, this is what we know," said Lieutenant Iraklidis, placing a file in front of him. "Symi police have detained two ladies, who match your friends' descriptions, on suspicion of murder and drug smuggling. Apparently, they drove to the police station yesterday, late morning, in a white pickup truck containing several boxes of ornaments packed with cocaine and a dead body. Symi police are investigating."

"What?!" shouted Matt and Demetrios together. "No, no, that can't be right, no they would never be involved in anything like that. This is all a mistake, it's not possible." Matt was getting more and more agitated by the minute.

"How well do you know these ladies?" asked Lieutenant Iraklidis.

"He hasn't known them for very long, Lieutenant, but long enough to know that they would not be mixed up in this kind of thing," Demetrios replied. "They are here for two weeks' holiday and were simply going on a sightseeing trip to Symi because they wanted to go to the monastery. Is there anything more you can do?"

"I suggest you get the ladies a solicitor." Lieutenant Iraklidis scribbled something on a piece of paper and passed it across the table. "This is a very good solicitor and friend of mine who I recommend you contact immediately. He will get the ladies out of the cells, if at all possible. I will tell you something now, but it must remain confidential between us. I cannot tell you all the details, but we are aware of drug-smuggling that seems to operate out of Symi. We have had our eye on several persons we feel may be involved, but until we get some concrete evidence, we cannot do anything further. It seems your friends have managed to get themselves mixed up with some very nasty people."

"Oh my God." Matt had turned quite pale. Although he had only known Donna and Fiona a few days, he couldn't just abandon them. He felt sure that neither of them would be involved in any of this and his urge to help was much too strong to ignore.

"I suggest you visit Spiros Galanis as quickly as possible," said the lieutenant, nodding towards the piece of paper that he had handed to Demetrios. "He will want to go across to Symi to get the ball rolling. He'll start his investigations and get the ladies out on bail if he can. In the meantime, I will place top priority on the case as this might be just the break we've been waiting for. I will telephone Spiros now and tell him you're on your way and fill him in on some background details. Try not to worry, we'll do everything we can to help these two ladies."

Chapter 23

Fiona and Donna had spent their first night ever locked up in police cells. They had some pretty close calls a few times during their younger days, but this time it was for real and of all places it had to be Greece! Donna reminded Fiona that it could have been much worse, they could have been locked up in the notorious Bangkok Hilton, which had an alarming reputation. Fiona simply reminded Donna that as they had never been to Thailand it would have been impossible.

A young police officer had brought them food and water, but the food was almost inedible and they left it untouched. They had no washing facilities, their clothes were dirty and they felt unclean. Their only toilet was a bucket in the corner. It was a good job they were extremely close friends and didn't mind peeing in front of each other. They were tired, hungry, filthy and extremely scared.

Officer Kallis appeared mid-morning.

"The body of Costas Papadopoulis has gone to Rhodes for post-mortem. We await results. For drug-smuggling you will be transferred later this evening." With that, he turned on his heel and left the cell.

"No, wait," yelled Donna, "you've got this all wrong. We've done nothing. The drugs were already in the back. Costas was just giving us a lift. Where are you transferring us to?

We're innocent. We've done nothing." But her shouting was a waste of time as Officer Kallis continued to walk away.

"Shit," cried Fiona. "We're never going to get out of here, are we?"

"Yes, we are."

"But how, Donna? Tell me how that's going to happen."

"Right at this minute I don't know, but we have to figure out some way to get ourselves out of this mess. You've got to stay positive, Fi."

"But nobody knows where we are, there's no-one to help us."

"Exactly, that's why we need to help ourselves," replied Donna. "So we'll have to take any opportunity we can when they move us later. But what's the betting that Kallis is in it right up to his filthy, stinking bloody neck and we don't know if any of the others are in on it as well. We can't trust any of them but we've got to get back to Rhodes somehow and find someone who can help us. We can do this, Fi. It will be OK in the end."

Fiona looked doubtful, but she was willing to try anything.

Chapter 24

The solicitor was waiting for them when Matt and Demetrios arrived at his office.

"Hello, I'm Spiros Galanis," he said, shaking their hands. "Please come in." He ushered them into his dark office, made even darker by two of the walls lined floor to ceiling with big, dark books. The two small windows along the third wall hardly let in any light at all. Spiros pointed to two chairs in front of the large oak desk that dominated the room and sat down opposite them.

"I have been speaking with Lieutenant Iraklidis and he has explained the situation to me. It seems as if your friends have got themselves mixed up with the drug-smuggling ring we are aware of. Can you tell me anything more that may be helpful?"

Matt went over his story once again, emphasising that the two girls would never willingly be involved with that kind of thing.

"OK, I can tell you I have put a call into the coroner's office and they have promised to let me have the results of the post-mortem on Costas Papadopoulis as soon as they have them. I can also tell you we have our suspicions about one of the police officers on Symi, but unfortunately, at the moment, we have no evidence to support that. That officer was the detaining officer in your friends' case. Time is of the essence. If I am to get your friends released, it needs to be before they bring formal charges against them, so I will leave for Symi now. Here is my card, with phone number. Please call me anytime."

"I'll come with you," said Matt, standing up to leave.

"I'm coming too." Demetrios stood and was ready to go.

"It is unnecessary for you to come, but I understand. I will go to the port and charter a boat to take us to Symi now. I hope you can cover these costs."

"Don't worry about the money," said Matt. "We'll find it somehow. We just want our friends safely back in Rhodes."

"OK, let's go."

The three of them jumped into the solicitor's car and Spiros drove quickly. Within minutes they reached the port, and Spiros quickly found someone willing to ferry them across to Symi immediately. He hoped they wouldn't be too late and the women already formally charged. But, if his suspicions were correct, the police officer involved would want to get rid of any potential witnesses as soon as he could, and Spiros felt sure he would only attempt that under the cover of darkness. He didn't want to tell these two men too much until he had the women safely in his care, and the sooner he got them out of that cell, the safer they would be. Spiros spent most of the journey on his phone, making one call after the other. There wasn't a lot of the day left, and he needed to get everything in place as soon as possible.

Fidgety and anxious Matt was at least a little happier that at last something positive was happening. Although he hadn't known the girls for very long, he had a strong feeling that they had already formed a lifelong friendship and he was happy to have them in his life, he didn't want to lose them now. Matt had always had intuitive thoughts about people throughout his life. He just seemed to know when people were genuine and would make good friends, and he knew when they wouldn't. His mother said it was because he was such a sensitive boy, but he liked to think it was because

CHAPTER 24

he was more spiritual and in touch with higher forces. He hoped these higher forces were with him now.

He willed the boat to move faster across the water, but it was going as fast as it was able and in less than an hour was docking in the harbour of the main town on Symi. The three of them quickly made their way to the police station, where Spiros approached the officer behind the desk.

"Good afternoon, I believe you detained two English women yesterday and I would like to know whether you have formally arrested them and what the charges are. I am Spiros Galanis, their solicitor," he said, handing the officer his business card.

"One moment please, I will find the arresting officer." The duty officer disappeared through the door at the back of the reception area. Spiros looked over at Matt and Demetrios.

"Don't worry, we're very close now to getting your friends back."

The duty officer returned, followed by Officer Two.

"The arresting officer is off duty I'm afraid, but this is Officer Giorgiou and he was involved in the detainment of the two English women yesterday."

Officer Giorgiou looked a little worried. Although the two women had been detained yesterday, nothing further seemed to be happening, and he wasn't entirely happy with the way Yiorgos Kallis was handling the case.

"Good afternoon, Officer Giorgiou. I am Spiros Galanis, solicitor for the ladies. Can you please tell me whether the women have been formally arrested and what the exact charges are please?"

"G-g-ood afternoon, Mr G-g-alanis." Nerves were getting the better of Officer Giorgiou, and he stumbled over his words. "The ladies arrived y-y-esterday in a white p-p-ickup truck c-c-ontaining a dead body and several boxes of ornaments filled with c-c-ocaine. They were both detained p-p-ending further investigations."

"And what further investigations have taken place over the last twenty-four hours?"

"This I cannot c-c-onfirm as it is Officer Kallis' c-c-ase, but I believe we have sent the b-b-ody to Rhodes for post-mortem."

"Have the women been formally arrested?"

"Ah, that I am n-n-ot sure."

"Well, can you be sure, please? You must have records on your system so please check."

Officer Giorgiou scurried across to the computer terminal. He knew he was on dodgy ground here, as he was sure that Yiorgos hadn't formally arrested the women, let alone updated the records. Yiorgos flew by the seat of his pants. He was not a team player and preferred to do things his own way rather than follow protocol. He expected the rest of the team to cover for him when the heat was on. Officer Giorgiou didn't see how he could cover his arse this time though, and decided honesty was the best policy. Plus, he felt sorry for the two women. He felt sure they were victims of circumstance rather than any wrongdoing on their part.

"Mr G-g-alanis, the records show that the two ladies have been d-d-etained on suspicion of m-m-murder and drug-smuggling, but as yet have not been f-f-ormally charged with any crime."

"Thank you, Officer Giorgiou. That is most helpful. As you have now detained them for over twenty-four hours without charge, I must insist that they are released immediately pending further enquiries."

Officer Giorgiou turned pale and looked flummoxed. He shifted his position to look at his colleague behind him, who slowly nodded his head. The desk sergeant knew that there was no reason to detain the women further, but wouldn't like to be in Giorgiou's shoes when Kallis found out.

Spiros walked over to Matt and Demetrios with a smile on his face. The pair had been observing the exchange and,

CHAPTER 24

although Matt had no idea what was being said, Demetrios was doing his best to listen and translate.

"They are now going to release your friends pending further investigation. I will tell you more later but first let's get the ladies and get out of here."

Chapter 25

Lying on her bed with her hands under her head, Donna was deep in thought. She'd been like that for the past hour. She couldn't understand why they were to be moved for the drug-smuggling when they hadn't been charged with any crime. Neither had they given any formal statement, and no fingerprints had been taken. She was certain Officer One was not to be trusted and had plans for them both, and equally sure he wouldn't make his move until after dark. They still had a few hours to come up with a plan of some kind. They needed to act before he could get them into a car and drive off to the middle of nowhere, but with nothing in the cell they could use as a weapon she wasn't sure how that would work.

"Fiona, are you awake?"

"Yeah, just lying here thinking about how we can get away."

"Yeah, me too. I think it's best we try as soon as Officer One comes for us. We can't let him get us in a car. Maybe we can both attack him as soon as he comes into the cell?"

"It might work. We would both have to be near the door as soon as we hear him coming, then we'll just have to jump him and hope for the best."

Fiona wasn't convinced it would work, but she didn't have a better plan. She didn't think the pair of them would be much of a match for Officer One. The only thing they had going for them was the element of surprise and the fact that there was two of them.

"Donna, you're shorter than me so go in low and hard, and aim for the balls. I'll aim for the eyes and nose. Once he's doubled over it will be easier to push him to the ground. With a bit of luck he will have left the key in the lock so we can get out of the cell and lock him in."

"OK," replied Donna, "that sounds good and to be honest I think that's the only option we've got."

"If we're lucky, we might just get away and find someone who can help us. That cop is such a shifty bastard, I don't trust him one iota."

"No, me neither," replied Donna.

They settled back down, thinking through their own part in their escape. It wasn't too long before they heard footsteps and a key inserted into the lock. The pair flew to the opening side of the door and flattened themselves against the wall. *Surely he wouldn't have come for us yet*, thought Donna, *it's still broad daylight*.

"Ladies, please to come with me." It was Officer Two.

The girls looked at one another in surprise. Donna briefly wondered whether he might be involved in whatever scam Officer One had going. He remained in the doorway so it was almost impossible to attack him. Fiona and Donna looked at each other questioningly, but Officer Two was already leading the way out of the cell and didn't try to restrain them in any way.

Donna shrugged as they followed him through the corridors towards the front of the building.

"What's happening? Where are you taking us?" asked Donna.

"Your solicitor is here and you are to be released into his care pending further enquiries."

CHAPTER 25

Solicitor, what bloody solicitor? Fiona kept her thoughts to herself.

They walked through the door to reception where Matt and Demetrios both leapt from their seats.

"Thank God we've found you at last," Matt cried, holding on to Donna. "We had no idea what had happened to you, but we've got you now and that's all that matters."

"But how? What's going on, and who's he?" Donna asked, gazing towards Spiros.

"Don't worry, we'll explain everything soon, but for now let's just get you both out of here."

They were both bewildered and had no idea what was happening, but Donna trusted Matt so complied. Spiros completed the paperwork before leading them down the steps of the police station and back towards the port area. His phone rang before they got too far.

"*Yassou? Nai, nai, entaxei.*" Spiros ended the call. "That was the coroner's office, Costas Papadopoulis died of natural causes, a heart attack to be exact. So there can be no charge against you."

"Can we go back to Rhodes now?" asked Fiona. What she really needed right at that moment was a long, hot shower and clean clothes.

"No, not a good idea. It may not be safe for you. Come, I have a boat waiting." He hurried them forward to the port and what, he hoped, was safety.

Chapter 26

They clambered aboard the waiting boat and settled themselves in the rear. Spiros explained that he was taking them to a safe place and that a very good friend of his, Nikos, had agreed they could join him on his yacht for a week or so.

"But why do we need a safe place, why can't we just go back to Rhodes and get on with our holiday?" asked Donna.

"I will explain everything once we are on the yacht, which is not too far away now. I will also need to take statements from you both." Spiros felt it would be better to do explanations once the ladies had showered and eaten.

"Ah, here we are," said Spiros, pointing to a 120-foot yacht that had just come into view as they rounded the headland. All four jaws dropped open.

"Oh-my-God," exclaimed Matt. "Is that for real?"

Spiros laughed. "Yes, this is Nikos' yacht. Nice, eh? His father gave it to him as a gift several years ago and now he spends the summer months on board. Nikos' family is extremely rich, his father is a Greek shipping magnate and Nikos works within the family business. Having the internet now makes it much easier for him to spend the summer months at sea whilst still doing business. He is a great host so you will have excellent hospitality with Nikos."

The small boat slowly drew alongside the yacht, lining up with the steps at the rear. After dropping off its passengers it turned around and headed back to its mooring in Rhodes. Nikos stood alone on the lower deck, waiting to greet his guests. *Blimey, he's every bit as gorgeous as his boat*, thought Donna.

"Welcome to my yacht," said Nikos as he helped the women climb aboard. "I am Nikos Laskaris and it will be my pleasure to look after you both until your predicament is resolved."

Spiros was the last to board, and the two friends greeted one another with a hug.

"Thank you, Nikos, for helping in this way, I don't have anyone else who I could trust enough to keep these two safe."

"No problem. Come up to the middle deck." Climbing the steps to the next level, the girls were dumbstruck by the luxury that greeted them.

"Please take a seat and I'll get you some drinks," Nikos said as he moved behind the bar and brought out bottles of beer for the men. "Ladies, allow me to show you to your cabins. I thought you might like to shower and change first. I'm afraid I have no clothes for you yet, but you will find bathrobes in the closets. Tomorrow, we will arrange for some clothes. Come."

The men made themselves comfortable on the plush grey cushions on the bench seating surrounding the stern section of the middle deck. They sipped their beers and chatted amicably while they waited for Fiona and Donna. But Matt was keen to learn what the plan of action was because, as wonderful as it seemed, Fiona and Donna couldn't stay on this yacht forever.

"You have your choice of cabins, ladies," said Nikos as he led the girls along a corridor, opening doors on the way.

CHAPTER 26

"We want to share a cabin, Nikos," said Donna. "We're not ready to be on our own yet. Is that OK with you, Fi?"

"Absolutely, I really don't want to be on my own either at the moment."

"That's fine, I understand. Then this is the best cabin for you," he said as he opened another door and ushered them inside.

"Oh my God," exclaimed Donna, looking around at the light oak wood and neutral shades of the soft furnishings. Nikos gave a quick explanation of the control panel set into the wide headboard spanning the width of the two single beds, and with the flick of a switch concealed lighting and strategically placed lamps came to life. Another switch closed the blinds over the large picture window and the view of the ocean beyond. Fiona gazed at the stunning artwork dotted around the walls, feeling sure they were probably worth thousands of pounds. Nikos opened the door to the bathroom.

"Bloody hell," said Donna, "this is bigger than my whole bedroom at home." She looked forward to a long soak in the full-size bath but for now it would have to be a quick shower.

"I think I've just died and gone to heaven," said Fiona, "this is pure luxury."

Nikos laughed, delighted that the ladies were happy with the cabin. He wanted their stay to be enjoyable, despite the circumstances.

"Ladies, I will leave you to shower and change. You will find robes in the closets. Please leave your clothes in the laundry basket and Maria, my housekeeper, will see to them for you. When you're ready, please join us on the terrace."

Fiona and Donna stood in the middle of the cabin, looking at each other. They couldn't contain themselves for long though and were soon jumping up and down, laughing and crying at the same time. Tears of relief flowed as they hugged one another.

"Right, get a shower first," said Fiona, "but don't be too long cos I'm desperate to be clean again."

Donna went into the bathroom but left the door open. She didn't want to be too far away from her friend and needed to hear her if she shouted. She turned on the shower, and as the hot water jets hit her skin, Donna finally allowed her tears to flow as she released the built up tension. The last twenty-four hours had been stressful and scary to say the very least and towards the end she feared for her and Fi's safety. At long last, she felt her body relax. They were both well and safe.

Finally washing her hair and body with the expensive bottles of shampoo, conditioner and shower gel on the shelf, she began to feel clean and more like her old self.

"Are you nearly finished?" Fiona wandered into the bathroom. She knew if she didn't chivvy Donna along, she would be in the shower for ages.

"Yeah, I'm done." Donna turned off the taps and took the large towel Fiona handed her. She wrapped herself in its big fluffy whiteness. "It's all yours now," she said, as she stepped out of the shower allowing Fiona to take her place.

Twenty minutes later, and they were ready to join the men. They found their way to the middle deck, and Nikos jumped up to make their drinks.

"Right," said Spiros as they moved over to the long dining table that ran parallel with the yacht. "First, I should explain that whatever is said here stays here. It must be totally confidential and does not leave this yacht. Agreed?" They all nodded their heads. "OK, good. Then, Fiona, Donna, why don't you two tell us step-by-step what actually happened." He pulled the notepad and pen towards him and was ready to take notes.

Donna explained what had happened from the minute they left the boat that took them to the island to when Spiros and the boys turned up at the police station. Fiona filled in with bits and pieces that Donna had missed.

CHAPTER 26

Spiros was scribbling furiously. He turned to Matt.

"Can you please explain your involvement in this?"

Matt told his story. Donna and Fiona were so grateful to him, if it hadn't been for that chance meeting on the flight to Rhodes, they could still be sitting in a prison cell, awaiting their fate.

"Now I will explain what I know. The detective you spoke to in Rhodes, Lieutenant Christos Iraklidis, asked me to help you. He explained that Symi police had detained two ladies for suspected murder and drug smuggling. He also said that the detaining officer was Yiorgos Kallis. The police have been watching Kallis for a while because they believe him to be involved in a drug smuggling ring, but have no concrete evidence to prove that, until now." He looked over at Donna and Fiona and smiled.

"I told you he was not to be trusted," Donna said to Fiona. "He's in it right up to his smarmy looking face."

"Fiona," Spiros continued, "you tell me he saw you watching him while he was loading the boxes in the van. Can you describe the van for me please, and the driver of that van?"

Fiona did the best she could, which wasn't much, really. All she knew was that the van was a dark maroonish-red colour, but she didn't get the registration number. She remembered a little more about the man and gave Spiros an excellent description, including the scar running from his eye and into the stubble on his face.

"Very good. And can you tell me again what Officer Kallis said when you next saw him, please?"

"He said someone would transfer us later this evening for the drug-smuggling."

"Did he formally charge you at any time?"

"No." They both shook their heads.

"OK, now that the police have a more solid case to build against Officer Kallis, I will work closely with Lieutenant Iraklidis and his team. With Costas Papadopoulis out of the picture, there must be someone working from within the monastery, so the police will need to investigate there. Once we know exactly who we're dealing with, we can hopefully confirm our suspicions and stop this corruption. Meanwhile, I have asked Nikos to keep you safe here on his yacht, as Officer Kallis will search for you both. He will want to silence you to protect himself."

Nikos was an extremely handsome man. In his early fifties, short dark hair greying at the temples, dark brown eyes lined with long dark lashes, and a lean and muscular body. Both Donna and Fiona couldn't help but feel the magnetic pull of the man. He turned to look at them and both felt their stomachs flip under his gaze.

"Ladies, when Spiros told me about this predicament that you have found yourselves in and asked if I could help, I suggested you come and stay here on *The Angel*," he said, with a sweep of his arm. "As far as we are aware, no-one knows you're here and we'll keep it that way. We'll keep moving around the islands and as far as onlookers are concerned, we are just a family enjoying their holiday. We will arrange for some suitable clothes for you tomorrow. Spiros will keep us informed of progress with your case and I am sure that Lieutenant Iraklidis will want to interview you both at some point, probably tomorrow. As soon as it is safe to do so, we'll get you back to Rhodes. In the meantime, I suggest we eat and then all try to get some sleep."

Fiona and Donna exchanged anxious looks. Although they were safe on the yacht for now, Donna realised the danger wasn't yet over. She reached out and took Fiona's hand.

"It'll be OK, Fi, this Detective Iraklidis will catch the slimy bastards and then we'll be able to go home. We can't worry about tomorrow, so let's try to relax and enjoy our time on this appropriately named yacht, our beautiful Guardian Angel."

Chapter 27

Yiorgos Kallis, Officer One, waited until past midnight before returning to the police station. He knew the staff would have left for the day, except for the duty officer at the front desk, and with a bit of luck he would be asleep as usual. If he used the rear entrance, he could reach the cells without being seen. Tobias had contacted the Albanians, and they were ready to collect the women from the port. It needed to be done under the cover of darkness, less chance of them being seen by prying eyes.

Kallis was happy with the plan and would be glad to see the back of the two meddling women. He didn't give a shit what might happen to them at the hands of the Albanians. That was none of his concern. If the truth be told, he cared little for people, anyway. He learnt at a very young age you couldn't trust anyone, not even your own family. As long as life was running smoothly and the money kept rolling in, he was happy. Everyone else took their chances.

He entered the door code into the keypad on the wall and slowly eased the door open, taking care not to let it slam behind him. Silently he crept along the corridor towards cell number one. It was dark, but he didn't switch on the lights in case the duty officer was still awake and came to investigate. He knew three of the four cells were empty, and he could see from the moonlight pouring in through the high windows that their doors stood open. Only the first cell was occupied. But as he drew closer he could see that door was open too.

He quickened his pace towards the cell, but the women had gone.

"Fuck," he exclaimed under his breath. He knew enough English swear words to let rip now and again. He stood by the door, running his hand through his hair, wondering what he was going to do next. The Albanians were waiting at the port and they would not be happy. They were a murderous bunch and he felt an icy finger of fear travel up his spine.

He needed to know where the women were, so had no choice but to go to the front desk and the duty officer.

"Constantine, where are the two women in cell one?" He didn't waste time on pleasantries.

"Oh Yiorgos, it's you. You made me jump, I thought I was alone here."

"I need to know where the women are."

"Why? It's the middle of the night. All I can tell you is that the case has been resolved and no longer a problem."

"Can you just tell me where they are?" Kallis was becoming impatient. Constantine was not getting to the point, and time was of the essence.

"I don't know where they are. They had gone when I came on duty. I didn't ask where, I was just told by the duty officer at handover that the case had been resolved and the women released, so no longer any of my concern. I thought you would be pleased."

"For fuck's sake, Constantine, this is important. Come out of the way and let me log onto the system."

Constantine was totally perplexed and wondered why Kallis was making such a fuss about the whole thing. He moved out of the way, he didn't want to get on the wrong side of Kallis and his temper.

Kallis logged into the system and typed in the names of the two women. As he read the report, the colour left his face.

CHAPTER 27

"You OK, Yiorgos? You've gone very pale." What was it with those two women? Constantine wondered.

"Shit," exclaimed Kallis, and quickly left the building.

Chapter 28

The Angel started a slow cruise back to Rhodes as soon as everyone was safely on board and finally dropped anchor off the coast of the Old Town. Spiros thanked Nikos for his hospitality and asked if one of the crew members could take him ashore. Matt and Demetrios felt it was time to leave too and the three of them climbed into the small vessel lowered from the rear of *he Angel.*

Spiros had a meeting with Lieutenant Iraklidis and Sergeant Doukas. Although he phoned the lieutenant as soon as everyone was safely on board, he only gave the key points. He now had to fill in the details.

After the men left, Donna and Fiona made their way back to their cabin. Nikos told them to treat *The Angel* as their home for as long as needed and explore at their leisure. They had a crew of four on board and Maria would take care of their personal needs. He gave them a slip of paper with a website address and some other details on it.

"I have placed a laptop in your room for your personal use. I'm sure you will want to let your families know you are safe."

"To be honest, Nikos, they know nothing about our little, er, misadventure. The police took our phones but we were so anxious to leave Symi we didn't wait to get them back, so we've had no way of contacting anyone. There's no point in worrying them unnecessarily." Donna didn't think it was worth all the stress it would cause Dave if he knew, much better to tell him when it was all over and they were safely home. She wasn't sure what Jeremy would do, probably fly straight out and demand that Fiona go home with him.

"Whatever, it's fine. But I suggest you use that website, log in with my details and order whatever you need for a few weeks." He handed Fiona a business card with the link to the store and handwritten login details on the back.

"If you do Click and Collect, Maria will pick everything up tomorrow. You will find some swimwear in the drawers in your cabin which were left behind by some, err, past friends. You may as well make use of them while you're here. It is clean, everything has been laundered."

"But can't we simply go back to our hotel and collect a few bits and pieces?" asked Fiona.

"No, at the moment it is better that you stay here until Lieutenant Iraklidis has solved the case. We need to keep you both safe."

"Blimey, are we really in that much danger?" asked Donna.

"Well, let's just err on the side of caution. But for now, have a good sleep and I will see you in the morning."

Nikos closed the door softly behind him and the two friends were alone. Fiona sunk down on one of the beds.

"What do you think we should do, Don?" she asked. "We haven't got any money, so can't pay Nikos for anything we order, and we can't pay Spiros' fee either. We can't expect them to pay for everything, they don't even know us."

"I know, Fi, but we have to take this one day at a time and just hope they will wait for payment until we're back home. Although I have no idea how I'm going to find the money, I will probably have to get a loan."

"Oh, don't worry about the money, Donna, I can sort that out, but my credit card was in my bag that Officer One took. I could try to log into my bank and do an online transfer, but

CHAPTER 28

I'm not sure I can remember my details cos they're all stored my laptop."

"We definitely need some clothes to wear while we're here cos we can't stay in bathrobes all the time. We can talk to Nikos about the money in the morning. Now I think we should try to get some sleep."

"Yeah OK. I definitely need some clean knickers, whoever pays for them."

Chapter 29

Lieutenant Iraklidis opened his front door and greeted his friend.

"Hello, Spiros, did everything go to plan?"

"Yes, the ladies are now safely with Nikos on the yacht."

"Good, good. Come on in and take a seat. Yiannis is already here. Can I get you a drink?"

"Oh, yes, please. A brandy would be nice, Metaxa if you have that?"

"Yes, of course."

Once they were settled with their drinks, Spiros felt the tension of the afternoon begin to ease from his shoulders.

"OK," said Christos, "what do you have so far?"

Spiros relayed what Fiona and Donna had told him. It was becoming clearer by the minute that something big was going on. Fiona's testimony would go a long way in nailing Kallis, but Christos knew he couldn't be working alone and really wanted to get to the brains behind this operation.

"That's all good," he told Spiros. "Once you phoned earlier and told me the women were safe, I put a couple of officers in place to watch Kallis and the monastery. I don't know whether anyone will make a move tonight, but it wouldn't surprise me. I don't want to miss anything happening. If Fiona saw Kallis moving the boxes into the red van, then he knows that her statement could be quite damning, and he will want to get rid of all evidence. With Costas Papadopoulis dead, who's transporting the drugs from the monastery? There must be a contact there, and tomorrow I will start questioning everyone. I have heard nothing from either team as yet. Do you think we have enough to convict Kallis with?"

"No, we don't," said Spiros. "We only have Fiona's statement, which, by itself, is nowhere near enough. If we can find the red van and the boxes, then we may well get fingerprints. You also need to trace the man with the scar who took the boxes. We need to gather enough evidence to pull whoever's working at the monastery in for questioning. He might talk or he might not, but I think that's the only way we'll be able to get a conviction on Kallis."

"Right, then that's what we'll do. Yiannis, you can come with me to the monastery tomorrow." Christos loved putting a plan into action. He really wanted to nail Kallis and had done for a long while. In his mind there was nothing worse than a rogue policeman. This was a colleague and someone you should be able to trust, so to put this smug bastard behind bars would be satisfying and would also help towards his promotion.

The three of them chatted for a while longer, but when Christos suggested another drink, Spiros declined. It was getting late, and he had to prepare for a new court case starting on Monday. He needed a clear head.

Spiros said goodnight to the two detectives, and promised to be in touch if there were any further developments.

Chapter 30

It was after three when Yiannis' phone woke him. He cursed as he reached for it and hoped it was important enough to drag him out of sleep.

"Yiannis Doukas," he answered.

"Yiannis, it's me," said Detective Iraklidis excitedly. "There's been a development."

Immediately wide awake, Yiannis was eager to hear what his boss had to tell him.

"The officer at the monastery has nothing to report, it's been quiet there all evening. But the officer tailing Kallis said he entered the police station just after midnight, using the rear entrance. He emerged ten minutes later alone but was clearly unhappy, kicking anything in his path. He leant against the wall to the building for a few minutes, running a hand through his hair; clearly a worried man. He made his way down to the port where a smallish vessel was docked. A torchlight flashed a couple of times as he approached. Two men got off the boat and a heated conversation took place. Unfortunately, the officer there could not hear what was being said. The two men then got back on board and the boat pulled out of its mooring, but not before our guy got the identification number of the vessel. Kallis returned home. Both officers are still in place and will report back if anything further occurs but, to be honest, I think that's all we're going to get tonight."

"OK," said Yiannis, "that's great. Let's hope the next report comes in working hours but it seems at least we are getting closer."

"Yes," replied Christos. "First thing we need to do is to try to trace the boat. Then we'll head to the monastery and start digging about down there. Can you organise a boat to take us to Symi as soon as possible?"

"Fine," said Yiannis, "I'll see you first thing in the morning." He ended the call and settled down for another couple of hours' sleep.

Chapter 31

S unday

The girls were up bright and early the following morning and felt much better after a good night's sleep in a comfortable bed. They found the swimwear neatly folded in one of the drawers. Donna plumped for a one-piece swimsuit in magenta with a flowery matching top which she hoped would help disguise her burgeoning curves, whilst Fiona, who still had an excellent figure, went for quite a revealing swimsuit and matching wrap in aqua.

Maria appeared in the corridor as soon as she heard their door open.

"*Kalemera,*" she called, "did you sleep well?"

"*Kalemera,* and yes thank you, the beds are lovely and comfortable," said Fiona, feeling refreshed after a good night's sleep and ready for whatever the day might bring.

"Yes, only the best on *The Angel.* Nikos is on the middle deck already and I'll bring breakfast shortly."

Nikos was sitting at the table, going through some papers and drinking coffee when they joined him.

"*Kalemera,*" he said, rising from his chair as soon as he saw them. "Did you sleep well? Please come and join me for some breakfast."

"Yes," Fiona smiled, "slept like a log, thank you. The beds are so comfortable but to be honest we were both so tired last night that I think we could have slept anywhere. Just knowing we were safe, and the gentle rocking was so soporific."

"You will be safe now. Yiannis and Christos will get to work and soon make some arrests, I am sure. But tell me, did you place your orders last night for the items you need?"

"We did, thank you very much. But I'm afraid we have no means of paying you at the moment. Our credit cards and phones are still in our bags at the police station."

"Please don't worry, you don't need to pay me any money. I'm sure these are just small things and I'm willing to take care of them."

Donna's eyes shot to the top of her head. *Bloody hell*, she thought. *He has no idea yet just how much we spent.*

"I can pay you back as soon as we get home," Fiona began again. Donna noticed her friend seemed quite animated and more verbal than usual.

"It is not important," said Nikos, waving it all aside. "Now, what would you like for breakfast?"

Maria appeared at the end of the table, ready to take their orders.

"Could I have some scrambled eggs and perhaps some bacon if you have it, please? Oh, and some toast." Maria nodded her head and looked at Donna. "Oh, I'll have the same." Tempted to ask for a full English, she thought that might look a little greedy.

"Would you like tea or coffee? Some fresh orange juice perhaps?" asked Maria.

"Tea for me and yes, orange juice would be lovely. Thank you." Donna loved her cup of tea, especially first thing in the morning.

CHAPTER 31

"Same for me, thank you," said Fiona.

"I'll have my usual, Maria. Oh, and can you bring a plate of fresh fruit too?" said Nikos.

"Well, ladies, your first day on board, but I'm afraid I can't offer you much in the way of entertainment. We cannot risk inviting anyone coming on board, so I'm afraid it will be just us. We have a small crew of four, the captain, the chef, a steward and Maria. I have business to attend to today I'm afraid, but I will join you later this evening for drinks and dinner. When you explore *The Angel*, you will see that we have a well-stocked library so please just help yourselves to any of the books there.

"The upper deck is the sun deck and has loungers. There are a few down here too, if you would prefer the shade. One of the crew will be around most of the time, so please ask for anything you need, or simply help yourself from the bar. Maria will go ashore later this morning and collect your order."

Blimey, Donna thought, *this man has thought of everything.*

Maria reappeared with their breakfasts. The girls were both surprised at how hungry they felt. Even Fiona, who was usually more mindful of what she ate because of her weight, attacked her food with a healthy appetite and enjoyed every mouthful.

"This all looks wonderful, Nikos," said Fiona. "How on earth does Maria manage to look after everyone and keep the yacht so nice all on her own?"

"Well, she does have some help," replied Nikos. "We make sure we head back into Rhodes Harbour at least once a month and have a team of cleaners come on board to do a deep clean. The majority of our groceries are ordered online and then delivered wherever we pull into port, or Dimitri will go ashore and pick up anything we need. Plus most of the time there's only me and if we have guests we get some extra help."

The three of them continued to make small talk whilst they ate, but eventually Nikos pushed back his chair.

"Please excuse me, I have to work now, but I will meet you here later. Is seven OK for you both?"

"Perfect," purred Fiona, as Donna shot her a curious glance.

CHAPTER 32

Officer Kallis was in a foul mood when he checked in for duty the following morning. He'd received a right bollocking from the two Albanians the previous evening, mainly for being seen by one of the women, but also for dragging them out on a wild goose chase.

They told him to find the women and stop them from talking, otherwise the entire operation was in jeopardy, and so was he.

Kallis had a sleepless night. He could have kicked himself for not formally arresting the women at the time. Even though he had no actual evidence, he could have thought of something. Now he had to come up with a plan to find and silence them one way or another.

Milos Giorgiou was at the front desk when Kallis got there.

"Morning, Yiorgos," Milos said cheerily.

"Why the hell did you let those two women go yesterday?" Kallis shouted at him in reply.

"I had no choice. Their solicitor turned up, and we had already held them for twenty-four hours without a formal charge. There was nothing on the system to show where we were with the investigation, so I had to let them go. Do you have evidence now to charge them? Here's the solicitor's business card. You can always call him and ask where they are."

"You had no right to interfere with my investigation. You should have checked with me before releasing them." Kallis snatched the card from Giorgiou's hand. *Fat lot of good that will be*, he thought, but pocketed it anyway.

What an arrogant bastard, what the hell was his problem? thought Giorgiou. He always knew that Kallis operated on a short fuse, but this was over the top. Giorgiou was only doing his job and didn't think he warranted such abuse, especially as Kallis hadn't even bothered to complete the report on the system. Giorgiou shrugged. *Sod him,* he thought and carried on with what he was doing.

Kallis stormed out of the building, wondering what gave everyone the right to interfere in his case. His only course of action now was to find the two women.

He walked quickly around the harbour, questioning the boat captains to see if anyone had seen the two women. Nothing. But a lot of the boats were out for the day already so he would have to come back later. The women couldn't have gone too far, surely. He questioned the shopkeepers. Nothing. He went into the cafés and finally struck lucky on the last one he tried. A waitress said she had seen two women and three men getting on a boat late afternoon time.

"What did the women look like?" he demanded.

"One had long blonde hair, the other was dark, but that's about all I can tell you. It was only a quick glance as I was clearing up for the evening. Oh, there was one thing I noticed, though. The men all looked smart and well-groomed, but both women looked a bit dishevelled, as if they'd not changed their clothes for days. I thought that was odd and couldn't understand why the women looked so grubby – it's usually the other way round. Does that help at all?"

"Which way did the boat go?"

CHAPTER 32

"I can't tell you that, sorry. I wasn't really watching because it was closing time and I wanted to get cleared up and go home."

"Yes, yes, thank you," said Kallis curtly as he strode off. Next was a visit to the harbour master.

"I want to know which vessels docked yesterday afternoon, times of arrival and departure, plus identification numbers. I trust you keep accurate records."

"Wait here." The harbour master went off to retrieve the log. He did not take well to the young officer's tone. A please and thank you wouldn't go amiss. He knew Officer Kallis well and that young man always had attitude. His lack of respect would not help his cause at all. Just because he was a police officer didn't give him the right to be so rude.

He took his time returning with the log.

"We have three entries for late afternoon. What exactly are you looking for?" The harbour master was equally abrupt. He didn't feel inclined to help this young upstart at all.

"Three men disembarked, the same three men plus two women re-embarked a short time later."

"Yes, I remember that," the harbour master said, as he wrote the boat's identification number on a piece of paper. "That was Vasi from Rhodes. He's in and out of the harbour on a regular basis."

Kallis snatched up the piece of paper and marched out of the office.

Ignorant pig, thought the harbour master.

Chapter 33

Yiannis Doukas had arranged with the port police for early morning transport across to the southern end of Symi. He knew his boss wanted to make an early start before the first boatful of tourists arrived on the island. They made good time and headed straight for the gift shop, empty except for a woman dusting ornaments.

"*Kalemera*, I am Sergeant Doukas and this is Lieutenant Iraklidis from Rhodes police," he said, flashing his police badge. "We wish to speak with the manager of this establishment."

She scurried off and a few minutes later a severe looking woman, dressed head to toe in black, entered through a door at the rear of the shop.

"Good morning, Lieutenant. How may I help you?" she asked through thin unsmiling lips, her hands clasped together in front of her.

"Good morning. I am Lieutenant Iraklidis, and this is Sergeant Doukas. We are from Rhodes police and investigating the death of Costas Papadopoulis, who I understand was employed by you. We need to interview your staff in order to piece together Mr Papadopoulis' last movements on the morning of his death. Could you please provide us with a quiet room for our interviews and have your staff standing by?"

"Yes, Lieutenant, please follow me."

She led them through to the rear of the shop and opened a door to a windowless and airless back room, allowing them to pass through.

"This will be adequate," said the lieutenant, "but please bring another chair and inform your staff that they will each be interviewed. We will begin with you when you return."

"Not much joy in her life is there?" said Yiannis, moving across to one of the chairs behind a scratched and rickety table.

"Doesn't look like it," agreed Christos, eyeing the piles of boxes and artefacts stacked precariously around the edges of the room.

Although the detectives knew Papadopoulis had died of natural causes, they had no idea whether he had any involvement in the drug racket. Investigating his untimely death was a perfect reason to interview the staff and should not raise any suspicions.

All the staff interviewed said more or less the same thing. Costas Papadopoulis was, by all accounts, an amiable man, friendly and would do anything for anyone. He was married with a couple of grown-up children. His job was to simply pick up boxes of souvenirs from the back of the gift shop and take them to the main town where they were distributed and sold around the tourist shops at the harbour. Some boxes even made their way to Rhodes and the mainland. He only made one delivery a day, and seemed content with that arrangement.

Christos knew they needed to pay a visit to Papadopoulis' widow before returning to Rhodes, so was eager to get on with the last interview. Tobias Panagos sat down, looking every inch a worried man. Although his statement was similar to the others, he couldn't make eye contact with either of the detectives and there was just something about him that didn't ring true. Both Christos and Yiannis felt he was holding back and, try as they might, they couldn't get him to talk.

After a brief visit to Mrs Papadopoulis to pay their respects and to sneak in a few well-chosen questions, they came away feeling no further forward.

"Well that was a waste of time wasn't it?" asked Yiannis as he settled himself in the rear of the boat taking them back to Rhodes.

"Yes and no," replied Christos. "I'm thinking Papadopoulis had no idea that he was transporting drugs, or if he did then he was very good at hiding it because not even his wife had any suspicions about him. The only one I'm not sure about is Panagos and I certainly want to talk to him again."

"I agree about Panagos but didn't the manageress strike you as a bit odd?"

"I understand where you're coming from, Yiannis, but no, I don't think you can take the severity of the woman as guilt. I honestly don't think she's involved, she's just one of those totally dark and closed people."

They both went quiet, lost in their own thoughts. Lieutenant Iraklidis hoped that, by the time they got back, one of the team had traced the small vessel that was met by Kallis.

Chapter 34

After a lovely, lazy day basking in the sun and reading books borrowed from the library, the girls made their way back to the cabin to get ready for dinner.

"I hope Maria has collected our order," said Donna. "I don't much fancy wearing the bathrobe again this evening."

"There's nothing here," said Fiona, opening the cabin door. She was disappointed. She expected to see bags on the beds waiting for them, but sadly nothing.

Donna went to the wardrobe to retrieve the bathrobe and gasped.

"Oh my God, it's all here." Maria had not only collected their order, but unpacked and hung everything in the wardrobe and placed the new underwear in the drawers. Like a couple of kids in a sweet shop, they couldn't stop themselves from pulling out the hangers and preparing to try on their new clothes.

"I'm going to have a shower first," exclaimed Donna. "I don't want to get suncream all over them, especially if anything has to be returned."

For the next hour they tried on clothes, running to the full-length mirror to scrutinise themselves and assess whether their bums looked big. They pranced around the cabin enjoying the moment and happy that nothing needed changing. Finally ready for the evening they made their way to the terrace to meet Nikos, who was already waiting there.

"Ladies," Nikos stood to greet them and placed a kiss on either cheek of them both. "You both look beautiful. I trust you're happy with your new wardrobe."

"Yes, thank you," said Fiona, "everything is absolutely fine, and it's so nice to feel normal again."

"What would you like to drink? Maybe you would like to try a Nikos Special this evening. A cocktail with a difference?"

"Oh, what's the difference?" asked Fiona.

"Now that I cannot tell you. It's a well-guarded family secret that was started by my grandfather. One day I might divulge the secret ingredient, but I will probably need to be held down first." Nikos raised an eyebrow and looked directly at Fiona, a hint of a smile on his face.

They chose the cocktails and settled around the comfy seating area. The yacht had dropped anchor for the night, and although they could see the lights from the shore twinkling in the distance, they had no idea where they were. It was a warm balmy evening, so typical of Mediterranean countries but rare in the UK. An orange glow from the setting sun had turned the ocean crimson. As darkness fell, soft lights bathed the terrace. It was perfect and both Fiona and Donna were determined to enjoy the moment, occasions like these rarely came twice.

"So, tell me a little about yourselves. Donna, what do you do back home?"

"Well, I'm a nurse at one of our major teaching hospitals in Cambridge. I got my general nursing degree at university, which is where I met Fi, and then went straight into a job in Addenbrookes Hospital in Cambridge. I took time out when I had my boys but when I went back, I specialised in cardiac care and am now a sister in the Cardiac Unit. I love my job, I love looking after people and making them well, but it's hard and stressful work with long hours. My real love

CHAPTER 34

is for holistic medicine and I love to combine some therapies with conventional treatments. The benefits to the patients are enormous and, on the whole, most of my colleagues are supportive of what I'm trying to do."

"Wow, Donna, that's so interesting. I would never have thought that you would be into that kind of thing," exclaimed Nikos. "What treatments do you use?"

"I mainly like to give Reiki, it's an energy therapy that balances the body, mind and spirit and is deeply relaxing. Touch therapy is also calming, especially at a time when patients are frightened and feel so alone. The results are amazing and patients who have the therapies usually recover a lot quicker."

"Donna is very good at what she does," chipped in Fiona. "She's very intuitive, although where that comes from and how it works is anyone's guess. She's given me Reiki a few times and I've always felt amazing afterwards. I trust her completely."

"And you, Fiona, what do you do back home?" Nikos asked.

"Well, sadly, nothing now. But I have a doctorate in Clinical Forensic Psychology and I worked within the police force before I had my children. Jeremy, my husband, didn't see any need for me to work again so I never went back, which I must admit I regret now."

"Oh Fiona, what a waste of your knowledge and expertise. Is there no way back for you now?" asked Nikos.

"Yes, I could go back tomorrow if I wanted to. I kept in touch with some of my colleagues, so I know the possibility is there. But it would cause too much fuss at home so probably best not to."

"Fi," said Donna, "I've told you before, just bloody well go back if that's what you want to do and sod Jeremy."

Fiona smiled wistfully at her friend. *If only it were that easy*, she thought.

"How lucky am I to have two amazing women on board. I salute you both," said Nikos, raising his glass to them.

At some point during the evening, Donna became aware of a subtle change between Fiona and Nikos. She thought yesterday that Fiona quite fancied the man, but she noticed that Nikos looked at Fiona for just a fraction longer than necessary when she was talking. Mind you, there was nothing not to like about Nikos, even if he wasn't so handsome there would still be something very attractive about him. He was a confident and self-assured man but completely without ego. He just oozed sexuality. She totally fancied him herself and, if it wasn't for Dave, she would be tempted.

The evening went by in a flash and it was late when they decided to call it a night. Back in their cabin, Donna turned to Fiona.

"So what's with you and Nikos then?"

"Nothing. Why?" replied Fiona, but she wouldn't quite look Donna in the eye.

"Oh, come on, please. I'm not blind. You've been acting all coy since yesterday. You fancy the pants off him, don't you?"

"Well, he's a very attractive man," Fiona replied.

"You wouldn't say no then?" Donna pushed, determined to get an honest answer from her friend.

"He hasn't asked, and to be honest, Donna, he's not likely to is he? He's simply being kind and helping a friend."

"I know he is, but you didn't answer my question. You wouldn't say no, would you?" Donna persisted.

"OK, no I wouldn't – would you?"

"If it wasn't for Dave, I wouldn't, no. But what about Jeremy?"

"What Jeremy doesn't know won't hurt him, will it? Anyway, you said whatever happens on holiday stays on holiday, right?" Fiona laughed. There was no hiding anything from

Donna, but she knew she could rely on her friend to keep quiet.

"Absolutely, you go for it, sugar, and just enjoy. My lips are sealed."

Chapter 35

Officer Kallis traced the identification number of the boat taking the three men and two women off Symi by searching the Coast Guard Documentation Database, and now had a name and address from the Registration Certificate.

His next job was to question the owner, Vassilis Thalasoss. Kallis needed to know whether Thalasoss had taken the group back to Rhodes or to an entirely different location. *Stupid mistake*, thought Kallis, *he's not bargained for me on the case.*

A quick phone call to the coastguard's office in Rhodes answered his question. The boat had already left its mooring for the day, but usually returned late afternoon.

Stepping from the Rhodes ferry later that day, Kallis headed for the coast guard's office.

"Where will I find Vassilis Thalasoss?"

"There," said the coast guard, pointing through the office window at the third boat along the jetty. Thalasoss was back and clearing up after a day of ferrying tourists.

"Vassilis Thalasoss?" asked Kallis, showing his police badge as he approached.

"Yes," responded Thalasoss, "how can I help?"

"You can tell me where you took three men and two women after you picked them up from Symi late yesterday afternoon."

"Ah yes, I remember. Strange group. Three men well dressed, one particularly so in a suit and tie, but oh the women. Dirty and scruffy and I had to wonder why the men would be with the likes of them."

"Yes, yes, but did you bring them back to Rhodes or take them elsewhere?"

"I took them to the big yacht. It's very expensive, probably costs millions. I thought surely not these women on this yacht with this man."

"And where was this yacht, and where is it now?"

"I don't know, it's gone. It was moored off the coast, in that direction," he said, pointing to the far horizon.

"Do you know this yacht?"

"Yes, everyone knows this yacht, it is *The Angel*."

Chapter 36

Christos and Yiannis met Spiros at a small restaurant tucked away along one of the back streets of the Old Town. Not only was the food better there, but it was half the cost of what the tourists paid in the prime locations.

"Do you have a table for three, somewhere where it's a little quieter?" Christos asked the waiter as they entered the busy restaurant.

"Is this OK?" asked the waiter as he led them towards the rear.

"Yes fine, thank you," replied Christos.

"This is better," said Spiros as he took his seat. "We can talk freely here without being overheard."

After a little friendly conversation, they made their food choices and ordered a beer each. Finally the lieutenant gave Spiros an update on what they had discovered.

"OK, so this is what we know so far," began Christos. "The small vessel containing the two men met by Kallis in the early hours is registered in Albania to an Erbardh Krasniqi. We've contacted the Hellenic Coast Guard for a list of the vessel's whereabouts over the past six months. We can widen that search period if necessary, but it's a starting point. So we now know that the Albanians are involved, but I'll come back to that later."

Yiannis continued with the update from their morning at the monastery.

"We interviewed all staff at the monastery and their stories are pretty much the same, Costas Papadopoulis was a good guy. His sole job was to take boxes of ornaments to the port in Gialos for distribution to the gift shops. We also spoke with his widow who, although deeply upset at losing her husband, did not indicate that he might be involved in anything illegal. However, one person did arouse our suspicions. Tobias Panagos matches the description given by Fiona in that he has a scar running from the corner of his eye and down his face. He works in the gift shop. His duties are to receive and unpack all incoming items for the shop and also prepare the items that Costas took to Gialos. He seemed very nervous the whole time, shifty, and couldn't look either of us in the eye. He also took a fraction too long to answer our questions. We can link him to Kallis so he is definitely someone of interest."

"Excellent work. We certainly have something to work with now. Have you heard from Donna and Fiona today? Are they OK?"

"Yes, I called Nikos earlier and everything seems to be OK on board."

Their food arrived and they took a moment to eat a little of the chef's speciality, lamb in the oven. It was delicious as usual.

"Tell me what you know about the Albanians," said Spiros, swallowing another mouthful.

"OK, we know Albania is a major player in the drug-smuggling network, bringing large consignments from Latin America to Europe. An international operation in over ten countries and lasting over five years culminated in 2020, when Interpol smashed what was probably their largest gang, the Kompania Bello, and made many arrests worldwide. Close to four tons of cocaine, with a street value of around five million euros, was seized over the period of the investigation. Now, we already know that when a major network is closed down, several smaller ones spring up and although what we have on Symi may be really small fry, it is still a problem.

"I have been in touch with Interpol this afternoon and am waiting for their man in charge to call me back. I have also been onto headquarters in Athens to alert them to the possibility that this operation could be more widespread across Greece. They are devising a plan of action, which we will, of course, be part of. At this point we have no proof that there are drugs at the monastery and that either Kallis or Tobias Panagos are involved in anything illegal. What we now need is the log of the Albanian vessel's movements and if that proves suspicious, I can get a warrant to search the monastery."

"Well, this is all moving quickly now, splendid work, Christos." The amount of information the detectives had gained impressed Spiros, and the knowledge that the Albanians were possibly involved was a major coup.

"Of course, from my perspective," he continued, "I am only involved in any implication of the two English women, and my chief concern is for their safety. I will, of course, do all I can to help close down any drug smuggling in Symi, and also here in Rhodes. Now that you can link Panagos from the monastery to Kallis it's a little easier to confirm the link to the two women, but of course we will need Fiona to give a formal identification."

"Yes, of course," replied Christos. "I too am concerned for the ladies' safety, but if we can smash this drugs operation then Kallis will be out of the way and the women will be safe. The sooner we can do that the better. But come, let's enjoy our food and the rest of our evening and I will update you again tomorrow."

Chapter 37

Officer Kallis felt pleased with himself. Never one to rein in his ego, he felt the need to tell someone how extremely resourceful he had been in tracking down the two English women. He called Tobias at the monastery and spent the first twenty minutes giving him a detailed description of exactly how he had discovered where the women were.

But then the Albanians cocked everything up.

All he asked was that the pair locate the yacht, pick up the two women and deal with them elsewhere. That would solve his problem once and for all. What happened to them after would be down to the Albanians and of no concern of his. All he needed to know was that they were out of circulation and could not testify against him. To be honest he didn't want to do the dirty work himself, and he knew Tobias would totally baulk at the idea of permanently silencing the pair. If only his stupid bloody police colleagues hadn't let them go, then he wouldn't be in this situation. It never entered his head that the fault was his, and if he had charged them at the beginning, he wouldn't have all this mess to deal with.

But the Albanians were not playing ball. As far as they were concerned the two women were Kallis' problem, one of his own making and therefore his to deal with. Although they agreed to take the two off the yacht, that was the limit of their involvement. They needed to get back to their gang on board the tanker as soon as possible and taking two women along was not an option. The tanker was coming in from Colombia, and it was imperative that they be at the rendezvous point to collect the next assignment. If they missed the connection, they would be in big trouble and heads would roll.

It had taken Kallis a while to come up with a new plan and although he was still working on it, he was getting close to a solution.

"Tobias, first you need to find a safe, secure and secluded place to keep these two women until we have decided what to do with them. I have spoken with the Albanians, who are in the process of tracking the yacht. Once located they will pick up the women, under cover of darkness, and take them to the cove. I need you to pick them up from the cove and take them to the safe place. I'll call you once we have located them."

No, Kallis was definitely not a happy man. The smug, self-satisfied feeling of the morning had disappeared, and all because of those two bloody meddling English women!

His day had not gone well.

Tobias wasn't a happy man either. It was one thing to put a few packets of drugs into ornaments, but another thing to keep two women against their will. This was all getting out of hand, and he really wanted no further part in it. But Kallis would never let him be free. The two Albanians were not friendly people either, and he didn't want to cross them. Tobias had no choice but to go along with the plan and set about preparing for the women's arrival.

He knew of a derelict barn that was isolated and not too far away, but far enough. He made a list of the items he needed to secure both the barn and the women, most of which were scattered around the monastery and at home. He knew that

CHAPTER 37

Kallis would never reimburse him so wasn't going to buy anything extra.

He wished he could find a way to get himself out of this mess. He was clear in his own mind, though, that he would not cause the women any harm. Oh no, that was not in his nature and definitely one thing he would not do.

Chapter 38

Monday

"Good morning, ladies," said Nikos, as soon as Fiona and Donna appeared on deck the following morning. "Today I have planned a little something to help relieve your boredom of being confined to *The Angel* and should be as safe as it can be. We will have lunch on a nearby island, at a small hotel run by friends of mine. Would that be OK for you both?"

"Oh yes, that would be lovely," said Fiona, always first to respond to Nikos.

"Good, that is settled. Dimitri will take us ashore in the small boat and pick us up when we're ready. I have some work to do this morning so will have to leave you to breakfast alone I'm afraid, but let's meet back here at twelve-thirty, if that's OK?"

"Nikos, this is very good of you. You have been so kind to us. I don't think we can ever repay your kindness," said Donna.

"Believe me, nothing gives me greater pleasure than being in the company of such lovely ladies," he replied, looking directly at Fiona.

After breakfast, Donna and Fiona took themselves up to the top deck for a couple of hours in the sun. They were picking up a good tan with all the sun and sea breeze, plus every now and again a quick dip in the ocean helped them cool off. It really was a quick dip too as neither one was fond of swimming, but there was nothing like the sea to help create that healthy golden summer look.

"You know, Don, I feel so completely happy and relaxed. I could stay here forever."

"Yes, well, a certain wealthy Greek not too many miles away wouldn't have anything to do with that, would he?" Donna asked with a smile.

"I can't deny that there is a strong physical attraction there," replied Fiona, chuckling. "But it's more than that, Donna. It's being here, with you, away from home. There's no pressure anymore, I can just be who I really am without worrying that I will upset someone. It's just so ... liberating." Fiona stretched her arms above her head and lay her head back as the sun's rays warmed her body.

"Are you really unhappy at home?" asked Donna.

"It's not that I'm unhappy as such, but I think these last few days have shown me that there's so much more to life. Even being locked up in a cell, and being here on the yacht for our own safety, is still better than being stuck in a humdrum life. But that's probably just the sun and the luxury talking, I'm sure once I'm back home I'll settle down again."

"Or maybe not," remarked Donna. "Have you ever thought of leaving Jeremy?"

"Oh no, I could never do that. Jeremy's not a bad man, Donna, he's never hurt me and he gives me everything I want. It's just that he likes everything to be a certain way and I just feel that somewhere over the years I've lost sight of me. Just ignore me, Donna, I'll be fine once we're home."

Mmm, or maybe not, thought Donna, but decided to keep her mouth shut for now.

Chapter 39

Detective Lieutenant Christos Iraklidis had slowly made his way through the ranks of the Greek police and was extremely happy with his current role with Dodekanissos Police Headquarters in Rhodes. Married, with two teenage children, he was a very happy man in most aspects of his life. Born and bred on Rhodes, Christos was one of six children while his wife, Helena, was one of ten. Together with siblings, spouses, children, nieces and nephews, their combined family was enormous and Christos loved nothing more than their many weekend get-togethers.

His rank as Detective Lieutenant suited his lifestyle exceedingly well. Crime on Rhodes was low and whilst it was on the rise, it was mainly tourist related and relatively easy to deal with. It was rare that he had to work evenings and weekends.

Whilst all of that was perfect, he often thought his mind wasn't being stretched as much as it could be and occasionally wondered whether he was becoming slightly stale and even a little bored. He sincerely hoped not because on the whole he was extremely happy, but he could just sense something niggling away beneath the surface.

Now he had a fresh case to deal with, and one that came by pure chance, he could feel himself beginning to fire on all cylinders. He was excited.

If it wasn't for that friend of Yiannis he would not be spending so much time at the station and loving every minute of it.

Helena, on the other hand, was not happy. Christos knew she liked him home weekends and evenings to complete her daily list of tasks and take her to visit various family members. He realised he would have some serious making up to do once this case was over, but in the meantime he, Detective Lieutenant Christos Iraklidis, was going to enjoy working on this case very much indeed.

Chapter 40

Christos had a very interesting phone conversation with the head of the Drug Trafficking Unit at Interpol's headquarters in Lyon, France. They were about to launch a large-scale operation aimed at smashing a major drug-smuggling gang operating mainly between Latin America and the Middle East. However, intelligence reported that there were several consignment drop-off points en route, with Greece being one of them. He suggested Iraklidis contact the Greek branch of Interpol based in Athens to see what the current state of play was.

His next call was to the superintendent in the drug-trafficking unit in Athens. Whilst they were fully aware of the gang and the major operation about to be launched, and knew of the Albanians' involvement, they knew nothing about Symi being involved. Iraklidis gave the superintendent the information he had gleaned so far, and they agreed to keep one another informed as things progressed.

He updated Yiannis, who was surprised at just how big this whole thing was turning out to be. Yiannis said he would inform Nikos and remind him just how important it was to keep the two women safe. In the meantime, Matt had gone back to England and Demetrios had resumed his flying duties, so at least Yiannis didn't have to worry about those two getting in the way. Although, to be fair, if it wasn't for them, he dreaded to think what might have become of Fiona and Donna by now.

Drug smuggling was a big problem for the residents of Symi. They had to put up with boats coming and going at all times of the day and night, plus Officer Kallis roaming gung-ho over the island. Their major source of income was from tourism and they couldn't jeopardise that. Although the police on Rhodes had received several complaints from the residents, there just wasn't enough evidence to do anything about it.

Christos thought that now was probably the right time to make his superior officer aware of everything, especially the pending Interpol operation, but he didn't want to scupper the whole thing by tipping off anyone involved. He decided to keep his own counsel for a few days longer and just wait for a further update from Interpol.

Chapter 41

Nikos appeared on the lower deck, looking very casual and handsome in a pair of jeans and a white open-neck shirt, sunglasses perched on top of his head. Donna swore she heard a throaty growl coming from Fiona.

"Are you ready, ladies?" he asked as the small boat appeared at the stern.

"Yes, we are. This is quite a treat, isn't it, Donna? Thank you, Nikos."

"My pleasure." Nikos jumped into the small craft and helped them both aboard. Once settled, they sped off towards the island of Leros, which they could see in the distance.

Nikos explained that Leros was one of the smaller islands in the Dodecanese and relatively quiet compared to Rhodes and Kos. Tourism was fairly low, but steadily increasing each year as people discovered its quiet charm. Today he was taking them to the Hotel Alinda, a small family-run hotel nestled in the Alinda Bay.

It was a beautiful location. The hotel overlooked the beach with an amazing view towards the medieval castle at Panteli. Although several people were seated around the bar and in the restaurant, there was plenty of space and Nikos chose a table with a stunning view through the trees lining the beach to the sea beyond. The purple bougainvillea hanging from the wooden structure framed the view, providing much needed shade from the scorching sun. It wasn't long before word got out that Nikos was in the restaurant and Mama, Papa, son and daughter filed out to bestow hugs and kisses upon him. He introduced Donna and Fiona simply as guests staying on *The Angel* and they too received a very special Greek welcome.

Nikos recommended the meatballs, the best in the whole of Greece he declared, and he certainly wasn't wrong. The three ate, talked, drank wine and relaxed in the warm afternoon sunshine.

"Fi, doesn't that man over there look like the man from Paris?" Fiona looked over to where Donna was pointing.

"Mmm, I can see what you're saying but no, not really." Fiona screwed up her mouth as she squinted at the man. She could see a similarity but nothing more than that.

"Who is this man from Paris?" Intrigued, Nikos wanted to know more.

"Oh it was years ago when we were at university," explained Fiona. "We were in Paris on the final stop before heading home and Donna noticed this man who always turned up wherever we went."

"That must have been quite unnerving."

"It was, Nikos, and more so because Fi couldn't see him for ages after I had. I thought I was going mad."

"Did you try talking to him, asking what he wanted?"

"I tried, but he always disappeared before I got to him. It was like he always knew what would happen next, or where we would be, and we just couldn't understand how."

"It got a little spooky," continued Fiona, "and in the end we went to the police."

"Fat lot of help they were," said Donna. "Apparently he hadn't committed any crime so they couldn't help, never mind the fact that he'd been following us all over Paris."

CHAPTER 41

"Did you feel threatened by him?" asked Nikos, fascinated by their story.

"No, not really," mused Donna.

"It was unnerving," continued Fiona, "and I wondered what his motives were, but he never did anything other than just be there."

"Did you ever find out who he was?"

"Sadly no," said Donna. "And this is the real spooky bit, the day we were going home we went to check in for our flight, only to be told the plane was full and we would have to wait a couple of hours for the next one. As we queued to go through security, I turned to say something to Fi and there he was."

"What, waiting to go through too?"

"No, just standing at the back."

"I turned round and could see him clearly," said Fiona, "which was the first time I had really seen him properly. It was so surreal, it was like the three of us went into a bubble, time just stood still, total silence, no people, just the three of us. Then just like that," she said, snapping her fingers, "it was over. I have never experienced anything like it."

"Suddenly it was noisy again and someone told us to move up." Donna gazed out over the ocean, lost in her memories. "He smiled, waved, then turned and walked away."

"And that was it?" asked Nikos, totally enthralled by the whole story.

"No, one more bit," Fiona carried on. "The next day my dad went out to get our daily paper and on the front page was a report of a plane crash killing all on board. It was the original flight that we were supposed to be on."

"*Skata*," exclaimed Nikos, "that is the weirdest story I've ever heard. You've never found out who that man was?"

"No," said Donna. "It was when I saw that man over there that the memories came back." They all turned to look where the man was sitting. "Oh, he's gone."

At the other end of the dining area sat two shifty looking individuals. Big and swarthy, bearded and decorated with piercings and armfuls of tattoos. Not the kind you would want to find yourself alone with down a dark alley. Although they were eating lunch and talking in quiet tones, they were observing the two women closely.

As soon as Kallis had given them the details of the yacht, the Albanians started their search of the area and that morning had found *The Angel* as it was dropping anchor off the coast of Leros. Keeping a safe distance they watched through powerful binoculars as the man and two women left the yacht and headed for the coast of Alinda Bay. Mooring their vessel alongside the small jetty, they set out on foot to track their quarry. It didn't take them long to spot the three in a restaurant by the beach, the perfect place to keep watch in broad daylight.

Several hours passed before they finally paid the bill and left. The Albanians did the same and sauntered back towards the jetty. They watched as the group made their way back to the yacht. The Albanians boarded their own vessel and pulled out of the bay, eventually mooring in the shallower waters between the yacht and land. One of the Albanians sent a quick message to Kallis telling him they had located the women and would collect from the yacht after dark.

They settled down for a long wait.

Chapter 42

The day was drawing to a close and after a lovely evening of eating, drinking and even a little dancing, Donna was feeling tiredness creep over her. She wondered whether she should just say her goodnights and let Fiona and Nikos have some time alone together. It was blatantly obvious that the pair were attracted to one another, she had seen the way they had danced together earlier. If she left them alone now, they might just take it to the next level.

Donna totally understood how her friend craved the excitement of this unknown man. He was one of the most attractive men she had ever met and it went a lot deeper than just his physical good looks. The man had a certain air about him that was quite irresistible, but he was totally unaware of just how bloody gorgeous he was and the effect he had on others. If she could bottle all of that, she would be a multi-billionaire by now.

She realised a long time ago that it couldn't have been much fun for Fiona being married to Jeremy. The man was a total self-obsessed arse who just wanted a trophy wife. The way he controlled Fiona was basically abuse, and she wondered why Fiona couldn't see that for herself. If Nikos could provide her with some escape, even for a few days or so, then who was she to stand in the way.

"What a lovely day it's been. Thank you, Nikos. I loved your choice of music this evening; I can never resist Abba's

'Dancing Queen' and just have to get up on my feet. But, I'm feeling completely knackered now," declared Donna, throwing in a yawn for good measure, "so I'm off to bed. Fiona, please stay and enjoy the rest of the evening, just don't wake me up when you come in."

She stood up and hugged her friend. As Nikos bent to give her a hug goodnight, she whispered in his ear, "Don't hurt her," and she returned the hug and left.

Fiona and Nikos remained on deck a while longer, enjoying a nightcap in the warm Mediterranean air and simply being in one another's company. Fiona told him she had two grown-up children who she adored but were away at university, so she felt a little lonely. She told him she thought she was more of an asset and a perfect hostess to her husband rather than any great love on his part. In her heart of hearts she knew they should have split up years ago, but they just plodded on out of convenience. She hadn't realised just how unhappy she had become over the years until this holiday with Donna had reignited that spark. Fiona told him of the fun times that she and Donna had together when they were at university, and how Donna had quickly turned into her best friend, and she never wanted to lose her. She laughed as she said that she would sooner lose her husband than Donna, but she knew that to be the truth.

Nikos told her he had never married and feared that time was running out if he were to ever find the love of his life. Although he had been with many women over the years, they all had the looks but that certain something was missing. He needed more depth to a woman than just looks. One of his biggest regrets was never having children. He told her how his father had built up the family business in the shipping industry and made a fortune. Nikos had wanted for nothing, his parents had given him the best of everything all of his life. He joined the business when he left university and now worked alongside his younger brother. Although he enjoyed the work, he felt that there may be something else waiting for him.

It was well after midnight when they ambled back to their cabins, neither one wanting the evening to end. Stopping outside Fiona's door, Nikos drew her towards him for a long, lingering kiss. Her head reeled, all her senses on high alert. The responses her body was making had lain dormant for years. This man was making her come alive, and she welcomed every feeling and sensation, every single moment. But somewhere some little voice warned her that this could all end in tears.

"Nikos, I ..." she gasped as she pulled away.

"It's OK, I understand, and I do not want you to do anything you're not completely ready for. But when you are ready, I will be waiting. Goodnight, my love," and with that he opened her cabin door and turned her towards it.

Chapter 43

Back in the UK Dave was becoming seriously concerned. He'd been leaving messages on Donna's phone for days and she'd not replied. It was unlike her. At first he thought it was just because she didn't have an internet connection, or the signal was poor, or she'd forgotten to charge the phone, but he reasoned that back at the hotel she would have all the internet and the signal she needed. He even checked on the hotel's website to make sure they had Wi-Fi.

She had sent a quick message they day she left to say they'd arrived safely and all was well. Then another a few days later to say all was good and they were off to Symi the following day for some sightseeing. And that was it, nothing since. It was nearly a week now since he'd heard from her.

He was looking at his phone as he walked into the lounge.

"Gav, have you heard from your mum since she left?"

"Nah, but then I wouldn't expect to. She'll be having too much of a good time with Auntie Fi to bother to message me. It's only when I'm out having a good time that I get endless messages from her." Gavin laughed, but he could see his dad was worried.

"Why, what's wrong, Dad?"

"Oh probably nothing, but I've sent her several messages just to check that she's OK, and I've not heard anything back."

"I'm sure she's fine. Have you tried phoning?"

"Yeah, but it just goes to voicemail."

"Why don't you try ringing Auntie Fi? You know what Mum's like, she's probably forgotten to charge her phone and it's as dead as a dodo."

"Good idea." Dave scrolled through his list of contacts until Fiona's name came up. He pressed call and listened as it rang. He was hopeful that she would shortly answer and confirm that all was well, but his hopes were dashed as it clicked to voicemail.

"Hers has gone to voicemail too."

"Well look at the time, it's nine here and they're a couple of hours ahead in Greece. So at eleven they will be in a bar somewhere and not hear their phones ring."

"You're probably right, but if I've not heard from her tomorrow I think I'll have to give Jeremy a ring and see if he's heard from Fiona."

"Good idea, Dad, but I'm sure you'll have heard from Mum by this time tomorrow."

Dave wasn't so convinced. Although he and Donna didn't keep tabs on one another, and neither were the possessive or jealous type, they still took the time for quick catch-ups when they were apart. It was just a thing they did to stop the other from worrying. This was not like Donna at all, and he was worried.

Chapter 44

The Albanians played the waiting game. They watched as the smaller of the two women left the terrace and shortly after a light came on midships, the same woman closed the window blinds. They hoped the other woman would be in the same cabin, their orders were to take both. Finally all lights, except for the regulation night lights, were switched off on the yacht.

They waited for another hour before they made their move. Nothing stirred on the yacht. Slowly and silently they pulled up alongside the stern, the first Albanian boarded and secured their vessel with a rope. With the second Albanian safely on board, they crept towards the cabin they believed to be occupied by at least one woman.

Both men were armed, neither one averse to using their weapons if they had to. Easing the cabin door open, the dimmed light from the corridor was enough to show both beds occupied.

Taking a bed each, they carefully made their way round to the side. With a nod of the head they made their move. Quickly and firmly the two big men pulled the women from their beds and, using the element of surprise, dragged them out into the corridor. Realising what was happening was real and not part of a bad dream, Donna started to struggle. With flailing limbs she put up one hell of a fight and soon tasted blood as she sunk her teeth into the hand clamped over her mouth. The Albanian cursed and tried to get a better grip but she was making enough noise to wake the dead.

Fiona used her long legs to push against the walls along the corridor, slowing their progress as the big Albanian kept losing balance, bumping into the wall behind him. Raking her fingernails down his face, his yell of pain pleased her.

The Albanians gave up trying to keep the pair quiet, speed was of the essence now. They were huffing and puffing with the effort, the sooner they got them off the yacht and fully secured, the better.

A cabin door opened and Nikos stepped out into the corridor.

"What the hell is going on here?"

The first Albanian had managed to get Fiona into their vessel and was tying her hands and gagging her. The second Albanian pushed Donna out onto the terrace and down the steps, finally pushing her roughly into the boat, just as Nikos made it to the top of the steps.

The Albanian turned towards him, drew his weapon and fired before jumping onto his own boat and speeding off into the night with the two women.

CHAPTER 45

They made it to the cove on Symi in just under three hours, keeping to a moderate speed. Tied with rope the women were bundled inside the small cabin area, out of sight. Their gags had been removed once they got going, but the bigger of the two Albanians was already regretting his decision. The tall blonde had not stopped crying since they left the yacht and the smaller dark one kept on and on and on, demanding to know where they were being taken. As if it was any of her business! He would either have to put the gag back on or knock her out!

As they rounded the last bend to the cove, a torchlight flashed on and off several times. Good, their contacts were in place and they could deal with these bloody women now. The larger of the two Albanians didn't know why they'd ever got involved with all this business in the first place. Their job was to simply deliver the packages, not abduct women. If it wasn't for that jumped up little police officer and saving his own arse, they could have been long gone. But here they were with these two troublesome English women. Well, that's the last job done, Kallis could deal with them now.

Donna and Fiona were pushed off the vessel and into the rough hands of two more men. *Sodding Officer One*, thought Donna.

"Hello, ladies," said Kallis, with a nasty grin on his face, "welcome back to Symi."

Bundled into the back of a waiting car, Panagos drove them to the shack in the middle of nowhere.

"You two," Kallis nodded towards the Albanians, "there's been a change of plan. I've spoken to your superior and your rendezvous has been delayed. You are to wait here for further instruction. In the meantime, you might as well be useful and guard those two. We will have a better plan in a day or two once I have spoken to your boss. Tobias will bring you food. Come with me."

"You bring beer too?" one of them asked.

"Yes, yes, beer too. Now come."

The Albanians were not happy, they thought their part in all of this was over. But at the mention of their boss, they complied and got into the car with Kallis.

It wasn't a long drive, but the constant bumping over the rough road was giving Donna a lot of pain in her back. It didn't take long before both cars pulled up in front of the wooden shack.

"Now what?" said Donna, as the girls were pulled from the car and marched inside. She was angry and becoming more belligerent by the minute, the pain in her back not helping.

"You have no right to keep us here, we have done nothing wrong so I demand that you release us immediately."

"Oh you do, do you?" Kallis replied as he started walking around the shack. "Well, let me tell you something. This is my island and I call the shots here. Because of your meddling you have made a situation far worse than it need be. If you had kept your noses out of my business, you would have been on your way home now, back to your rain-soaked country. But no, you had to poke your noses in and now we all find ourselves in an unfortunate situation, and one that I have to deal with – but not tonight. I suggest you make yourselves comfortable." Kallis turned and left the shack with Tobias close on his heels.

"Now what?" asked Tobias once they were outside.

CHAPTER 45

"I don't bloody know," replied Kallis as he wiped a hand across his troubled face. "Tomorrow I will have a plan, but now it's late and I can't think straight. The Albanians have totally let me down."

Chapter 46

Michalis, captain of *The Angel*, was the first to arrive on the middle deck. Awoken by the sound of a gunshot he knew that something was seriously wrong and, banging on his fellow crew members' cabins as he passed, he made it just in time to see the Albanians' vessel speeding away.

Nikos was lying on the floor, blood seeping from his upper body and pooling around him. Michalis quickly took control of the situation, barking instructions to the others.

"Dimitri, contact the hospital and the police. We need urgent medical help for a gunshot wound. Give them our exact location. Maria, press here and try to stem the flow of blood. Elias, check on the two ladies."

Michalis looked down at his friend. The loss of blood from a chest wound had drained his face of colour. He feared the worst but hoped and prayed that Nikos would make it. Michalis had known Nikos since they were children and he was one of his oldest and dearest friends. A few years back Nikos had asked if he would be interested in the captaincy of *The Angel* and made him an offer he couldn't refuse. Growing tired of his long and distinguished career on the cruise liners, he welcomed the chance of something closer to home and seeing more of his family. The last few years with his friend had been some of his happiest and he couldn't bear to think of losing him now.

"Come on, Nikos," he said as he brushed the hair back from his face. "Stay with me. Help is on the way, just stay with me, my friend."

"The women have gone," said Elias rushing back to the deck. "I've searched the entire yacht and they are nowhere."

"I thought as much," replied Michalis. "When I arrived here, I saw a boat disappearing in that direction. My guess is they came for the ladies."

It seemed an age before they heard the rhythmic whoosh of helicopter blades in the distance. The thudding grew louder until finally hovering over the yacht a figure appeared at the opened doorway. The rotor blades created a strong downdraft causing the paramedic to swing precariously as he was slowly lowered to the deck. The cable was quickly winched back and a second figure appeared. The two medics worked quickly and expertly, stabilising Nikos. With the help of oxygen and intravenous fluids they were finally satisfied and Nikos was secured on a stretcher and winched safely into the helicopter.

"Maria, go and get changed quickly and go with him. I will wait for the police to arrive, but please keep us updated." Michalis looked questioningly at the second medic, who nodded. As soon as Maria returned the medic started attaching a harness to her and once they were both secured, he gave the thumbs-up signal and they were winched up together. Maria held on tightly and closed her eyes. The pair lurched from side to side as the air caught them. Finally safely on board, the helicopter flew off taking Nikos to the hospital in Leros for emergency treatment.

Police officers from Leros arrived in a police launch about ten minutes later. Michalis took them into the inside lounge and gave an account of what had happened.

"There's a lot of background to this so it's not as simple as it seems," he said. "I don't have all the details so suggest you contact Lieutenant Iraklidis in Rhodes."

CHAPTER 46

The officers took details from the rest of the crew and left, with the promise that they would inform Rhodes police of the situation and begin the search for the vessel and the two missing women.

With just the three crew left on board, they knew any further sleep would be impossible so settled in the lounge to await the news from Maria at the hospital.

Chapter 47

"What the bloody hell have we got ourselves into?" Fiona asked.

"I don't know," said Donna, "but it's not looking good."

"They shot Nikos." Sobs wracked Fiona's body. She felt guilty they had involved him in something so dangerous when all he was trying to do was help them.

"I know, darling, and I'm so very sorry. But you must stay positive. He may be OK, the bullet might have missed or just nicked his arm or something simple like that."

"No, it's more serious than that. I saw him fall backwards. Oh Donna, what the hell do we do now?"

"We need to come up with a plan; we've done it before and we can do it again." Donna sounded a lot more confident than she felt. Any action was better than no action, so she thought about their options.

Being tied up was not helpful. Movement was restricted as their hands were tied behind them and feet now bound at the ankles. Shuffling about on their bums they managed to manoeuvre so they were sitting back-to-back; hopeful they could untie each other's ropes. It wasn't easy. The tightness of the binding was already turning Donna's hands numb and she had to keep stopping to rest her arms. Hope drained away from her, and her thoughts drifted to Dave and her boys.

"Donna, this is all so bloody useless. It's pitch black in here and even if we could see what we're doing, these ropes are so tight I'm not sure we could undo them."

"I know," replied Donna. "I don't think we have any choice but to wait until those bastards come back and then see what happens."

Chapter 48

Tuesday

"Yes," Lieutenant Iraklidis answered half asleep. He peered at the bedside clock, still a couple of hours before the alarm went off at seven.

"This is Officer Ariti of Leros police. At approximately three this morning we received an emergency phone call from the yacht *The Angel* claiming that a man had been shot and two women abducted. We boarded the yacht and can substantiate the report. During the process we were given your name as the lead detective in charge of a large operation involving the victims."

"Yes, correct. Who was shot, and do you have any idea who took the women and where they were taken to?"

"Nikos Laskaris sustained a gunshot wound to the chest and is now undergoing emergency surgery at the hospital here in Leros. We don't know who took the women or their current whereabouts. Members of the crew reported that two men boarded *The Angel*, Mr Laskaris was in pursuit when one man fired the shot."

"OK, thank you. I am on my way. Please do not let *The Angel* move from the area."

Christos Iraklidis ended the call and immediately phoned Yiannis.

"What's going on? Who was that on the phone at this time of night? Christos, what's happening? It's woken me up," complained Helena.

"Ssssshhhh, I'm on the phone. It's police business. Go back to sleep, Helena."

Christos climbed from his bed. He had to make a phone call and then go to work, but he didn't want to disturb Helena unnecessarily.

Yiannis answered his phone.

"Yiannis, it's Christos. We have a situation, I'm afraid. I have just taken a call from Leros police. The two English women have been abducted from the yacht and Nikos has been shot. I am leaving for Leros now."

"OK, I'm on my way and will meet you at the port."

Chapter 49

"Hi Dad, alright?" Gavin had just come home from a busy day sorting out the electrics in a big old Victorian house being converted into apartments.

"Hi Gav, yeah I'm OK but I've still not heard from your mum."

"Have you tried calling her again?"

"Yes, but it's still going straight to voicemail."

"Mmm, strange even for Mum."

"I think I'm going to phone Jeremy." Dave didn't want to have to resort to that but he didn't think he had much choice. He didn't care for Jeremy at all, in his mind he was a jumped up pompous prick who cared for no-one but himself. He didn't think he'd get much joy from him either but it would set his mind at rest if he'd heard from Fiona and knew that the girls were OK.

Their house phone rang and rang until the answerphone cut in. He didn't bother to leave a message, he knew that Jeremy would never return his call. He didn't have Jeremy's mobile number, there had never been any need because they had never been, or likely to be, friends. He'd have to keep trying the house phone until he finally got an answer.

"Do you want to go down the pub for something to eat, Dad? Mark is seeing some new girl tonight and Tom is out with his mates, so it's just me and you."

"Yeah, OK and then by the time we get back Jeremy should be home."

Stuffing phones, keys and wallets into their pockets, they walked the short distance to their local in the centre of the village. The pub was the hub of village life, everyone knew everyone and there was always someone to chat with. It was one of the nice things about living in a small village but it could also be a curse, not much remained private. It took Dave and Gavin several minutes of pleasantries before they finally reached the bar and ordered drinks and food.

By nine Dave was more than ready to get back home and try Jeremy again. Gavin, beginning to share his dad's concern about his mum, was ready to call it a night too.

Luck was on Dave's side as Jeremy answered on the third ring.

"Hello, Jeremy, it's Dave Chambers here, Donna's husband. I'm just wondering if you've heard from Fiona since the girls have been away?"

"Er no, should I have?"

Bloody hell, thought Dave, *he's still a belligerent prick.*

"I just wondered, that's all. I've not heard from Donna for over a week and it's not like her at all."

"Well, have you tried phoning her?"

"Yes, Jeremy, of course I have. Both their phones go straight to voicemail. I just thought you might have heard from Fiona, but I'm sorry I bothered you."

"This would never have happened if Fiona had just done as I said and stayed at home."

CHAPTER 49

"Well quite frankly, Jeremy, the girls are old friends and really don't need anyone's permission to go off on holiday together. But hey, I'm sure they're fine so don't let my phone call concern you at all." Dave hung up before Jeremy had a chance to reply.

"What a complete and utter arsehole." Dave didn't know what he should do next, but knew he needed to do something.

"Why don't you phone their hotel in Rhodes? They'll know where they are and can probably put you through to their room."

"Good idea, Gav, I'll find the phone number. I know your mum wrote it on a bit of paper before she left. It's probably on the board in the kitchen."

Twenty minutes later Dave was no further forward.

"They're not at the hotel," he said, as he walked back into the lounge. "What's more, they've not been back since they left for Symi over five days ago. Now I'm seriously worried."

"What are you going to do?"

"I don't have a choice, I'm phoning the police."

CHAPTER 50

Yiannis Doukas was in his thirties, unmarried and didn't have to worry about anyone else in his life. He was unsure if he was happy with that or not. Some days yes, other days not. He had a wonderful group of friends, and his social life was great, but life could get lonely without someone special to share it with.

Yiannis was confused about his sexuality. He always thought he was straight and had a few girlfriends over the years, but then along came Demetrios several years back and it threw him into turmoil. He knew Demetrios was gay. Demetrios never tried to hide the fact, and it was refreshing to see somebody totally confident with who they were. But Yiannis had developed a bit of a crush on him, and now he didn't know who he was supposed to be. Was he gay, was he straight, was he bi? How the hell was he supposed to know?

It would mortify his parents if he turned out to be anything other than what they wanted him to be, especially his mother who was already reminding him it was about time he married and gave her a brood of grandchildren.

It was not something he could talk about with anyone, really. His friends all thought of him as straight, and he wondered if they could ever accept him as anything else. His life was plodding along quite smoothy until Demetrios turned up in his office the other day with a handsome Englishman and now his thoughts and feelings were all over the place again.

He needed to concentrate on his work. The current case was quite challenging and he was loving every minute. He had hopes of rising through the detective ranks and maybe one day moving from Rhodes to Athens, where the crime rate was a lot higher and the cases more interesting.

Maybe it was better to stay free and single, for the time being, anyway. Hopefully, he would just know when the right person came along, whatever gender they may be.

In the meantime, he needed to put all thoughts of Demetrios out of his mind and concentrate on the current case, and they needed to find the two women before it was too late.

Chapter 51

Wednesday

Christos found Yiannis standing next to the police launch on the quayside the following morning.

"Morning, boss," said Yiannis.

"Morning. OK, so this is what we have so far," said Christos, as he took his seat in the launch and repeated the earlier conversation with Leros police.

"I phoned my contact at Interpol, who told me they were about twenty-four hours away from launching their operation but with the kidnap of the two British women they may well bring it forward. He will phone me again in about an hour."

"OK," said Yiannis, "so in the meantime, how do we find the ladies? I am very concerned for their safety."

"Me too, Yiannis, me too. The only connection we have is Symi, Kallis and the monastery but of course, they could have taken the women anywhere. I'd put money on Kallis being involved though."

"Kallis has to be involved," replied Yiannis. "He saw Fiona watching him transfer the boxes to the red van, so he knows she is a witness. She can also identify the other man involved who may, or may not, be Panagos from the monastery. We need to find the red van and the boxes and dust them for fingerprints, if they've not already been shipped elsewhere."

"Agreed. Get someone on the search, can you. I think we'll also pay Officer Kallis a visit, if nothing else it may ruffle his feathers a bit."

Chapter 52

It was daylight when Donna opened her eyes. She was not sure how it had happened, but she had slept for a couple of hours and Fiona still had her eyes closed.

Fear kicked in as she looked around the derelict wooden structure. She had no idea where they were and she didn't know how they could get out of it. What the hell had they gotten themselves involved in? she wondered. The only positive thing about Nikos being shot was that by now the police would be involved and hopefully trying to find them. She hoped and prayed that he hadn't been too badly hurt. Fiona would be an utter wreck if their kidnappers had killed him.

She reasoned Kallis would be back sometime during the day, and God only knew what he had in store for them. She hoped he might untie them so they could have at least half a chance of getting away, but there was nothing in the empty shack that she could see that would make a useful weapon. Daylight was seeping through the cracks of the walls. Donna could see gaps between some of the wooden slats and wondered how easy it would be to pull a few away and escape through the gap. Although where they would escape to was anyone's guess.

She could hear voices outside. Rough voices and in an unfamiliar accent. She didn't recognise the language but was certain it wasn't Greek. Must be the Albanians, she thought.

What were they doing outside? Would they come inside the shack? A new fear suddenly crept into her mind. Not only could these men murder them, but they could beat and rape them too.

Fiona stirred.

"Jeez, Donna, I could really do with a wee."

"Well, you'll just have to go where you are."

"You mean just pee myself?" said Fiona, absolutely horrified at the thought.

"Yes, Fiona, just pee yourself. What choice do you have? Unless you've not noticed there are no bathroom facilities. And even if there were you couldn't use them because you're tied up!"

Donna was feeling the strain of it all and knew that she was being snappy with Fi, and that was completely unwarranted. There was nothing either of them could do except sit and wait. Unless …

"Fiona, you do yoga and Pilates, don't you?"

"Yes."

"So would you say your body is quite flexible?"

"Yes, I suppose it is. Why, are you thinking of taking up yoga when we get home?" Fiona was puzzled. Why on earth would Donna be thinking of joining a yoga class when they had just been abducted, tied up and dumped in this godforsaken sodding hole.

"I'm thinking, could you bring your arms down under your bum and then down the backs of your legs and out under the bottom of your feet so they end up in front of you?"

"I could try, but what good will that do? I'll still be tied up."

"Yes I know, but you'll be able to see what your hands are doing and you might be able to untie me." Donna shook her head in despair. *For such an intelligent woman, Fiona could really border on stupid at times*, she thought.

"OK, I'll give it a go."

Fiona shuffled. She grunted and groaned with the effort. She moaned in pain as the ropes dug deeply into her wrists. Slowly she manoeuvred her hands down to her bottom. Donna couldn't see what was happening as they were still back-to-back, but she heard enough to know that this was no easy feat for Fiona, as supple as she was. Two more shuffles and Fiona was sitting on her hands. She stopped and rested for a minute or two hoping that the pain in her shoulders would soon start to ease. Another couple of shuffles and her tied hands were under her thighs. They hurt like hell, especially where the ropes had rubbed her wrists raw, but she took a deep breath and carried on. Inch by inch, she slowly brought her hands down and drew her knees up towards her body. Another pause. *Nearly there*, she thought as she lifted her legs and then slowly toppled over onto her side.

"Bugger," she exclaimed. "Donna, I've fallen over. I was almost there."

"OK, just rest a minute and then try to get your hands over your feet while you're lying down, it might be easier."

She took a moment to prepare herself. With a deep breath she quickly brought her knees close to her chest as she slipped her arms under her feet and to the front of her body. Donna heard her cry out in pain.

"Fiona, are you OK?"

"Oh my God, I've done it, Donna, my hands are in front."

"Oh, brilliant, Fi, just absolutely brilliant. Well done, darling. Just lie there a minute and catch your breath. When you're ready try and sit up and then let's shuffle around so you can try to untie me."

Five minutes later Fiona had managed to push herself up and was sitting with her hands in front of her. Although the acute pain had eased, her limbs still ached and her wrists were bleeding and sore. It was easier now that Fiona could see what she was doing, but the ropes were so tight she hardly made any headway in loosening them. Progress was slow, but encouraged by Donna, she just kept going.

They both froze when they heard the vehicle pull up outside the shack.

Chapter 53

The journey to Leros seemed to take forever but Christos and Yiannis finally arrived late morning. The young officer who Christos had spoken to earlier met them at the port in Lakki and took them straight to the hospital to check on Nikos. Christos sighed; he sincerely hoped Nikos was not too badly injured, especially as he had gone out of his way to help with the two ladies. The last thing he needed right now was for this to turn into a murder investigation.

It was a quick ride from the port and in a few short minutes the pair were striding up to a small reception window. An elderly woman peered at them over her glasses. Yiannis showed his police ID and asked for an update on Nikos Laskaris. Eventually the older lady found someone to take to the visitors' room. They were shown into a large waiting area and told a doctor would be with them shortly. Anxious relatives filled the rows of seats, Maria was one of them.

She was on her feet and rushing towards them as soon as they came through the door. She recognised Yiannis from his brief visit to *The Angel*, but she didn't know the other man.

"Hello, Maria," Yiannis greeted her, noticing how exhausted she looked. "This is Lieutenant Christos Iraklidis from Rhodes. Boss, this is Maria who works with Nikos on board *The Angel*. Maria, how is Nikos?"

"I don't know. I've been waiting since we arrived but I've seen no-one. I am so worried, that man shot him and there was so much blood." Tears formed in Maria's eyes. Yiannis put an arm around her shoulders and comforted her as best he could.

"We should have news soon, and if not, I will find someone who can give us an update. While we wait, I think Lieutenant Iraklidis would like to ask you a few questions, if that's OK with you?"

"Yes, of course," replied Maria. "I want these men caught. They have our two ladies, you must find them."

"Maria, may I call you Maria? I am Christos Iraklidis and we are investigating a major crime in which the two English women have somehow become involved. We believe them to be completely innocent, but there are others who think they know too much. Nikos Laskaris agreed they should stay on the yacht for their own safety until we have concluded our investigations. Unfortunately, the criminals discovered their whereabouts, which led to their abduction and the subsequent shooting of Mr Laskaris. Now, Maria, I would like you to tell me exactly what happened from the moment you knew something was wrong until now."

Maria nodded and told her story, which really wasn't very much at all. By the time she reached the lower deck Nikos had already been shot and was lying on the floor. She could remember a boat speeding away, but her description of it was vague.

Five minutes later a doctor appeared, still in his scrubs. All eyes were on him.

"Nikos Laskaris?" he called, and Yiannis, Christos and Maria stood and moved towards him. Christos showed his ID card and made the introductions.

"Nikos is out of surgery and is one very lucky man. Although the bullet penetrated the chest, it missed all vital organs and lodged in the rhomboid major muscle in the back. He will have limited movement while it heals and it will be

CHAPTER 53

uncomfortable but, in time, we are sure he will make a full recovery. We have removed the bullet and have bagged it. I will make sure it is handed over to you, Lieutenant."

"Thank you very much, Doctor, may we see him?" asked Yiannis.

"Yes, he is awake. But please do not stay too long, he is tired and very weak. We will keep monitoring him and all being well, he can possibly go home in a few days. But he will need some care."

"I will look after him, Doctor," said Maria, smiling for the first time in many hours.

Chapter 54

Kallis was in one hell of a foul mood.

Fucking Albanians. Why couldn't they just do the whole fucking job? Useless fucking bastards. They couldn't organise a piss-up in a brewery. Good job I'm here to get things done, otherwise we'd all be up shit creek.

He paced up and down his apartment. He needed to get rid of these women and it needed to be done today. It was no good asking Tobias to do the job, even if he were to agree he would cock it up somehow. He could pay someone to do it, but that would be another potential witness against him, and he really didn't want to spend that much money on dealing with a couple of loose ends. No, like it or not, he would just have to do the job himself.

This was a first for him, he'd never killed before. Yes, he'd done some pretty nasty stuff in his time but always got someone else to do the real dirty stuff.

He considered his options.

He could shoot them but then the bullets could be traced to his own police service firearm. Unless he said his firearm had been stolen. But that would start a whole web of lies that had the potential to trip him up. No, shooting was out of the question.

He could use a knife, but that would leave blood to clean up and blood always left a trace, however well it was cleaned.

He could hit them over the head with a heavy object, but again there was the potential for blood. Plus he couldn't be sure that one blow would be enough.

The best and cleanest way would be to strangle them. Difficult. There would be a struggle, but possibly less incriminating to him. He didn't relish this though; not as quick as he would like. Still, it couldn't be helped.

But then he still needed to get rid of the bodies. By far the easiest and quickest way would be to take them out to sea and toss them overboard. He would have to add weights, of course, to stop them floating up and eventually drifting to the shore.

No, Officer Kallis was not a happy man at all. He didn't understand why those bloody Albanians hadn't just chucked them overboard when they had the chance.

And then the lightbulb moment came.

It would have to wait to the following night as he was on duty that evening, but another 24-hours wouldn't matter.

He phoned Tobias.

"Tobias, I need a boat to be ready at the cove just after midnight tomorrow night. Bring the women and a torch and a sharp knife. We're all taking a little night fishing trip."

"No, no," said Tobias. "I want nothing to do with this."

"You will, Tobias, you will be there and you will do exactly as I say."

"Please, I do not want to hurt anyone," a pleading note crept into Tobias' voice.

"Tobias, do not make me get angry with you. I have enough evidence on you to put you away for a long, long time. Or I could simply hand you over to the Albanians. Which would

CHAPTER 54

you prefer? Be there tomorrow just after midnight or you face the consequences."

Kallis was pleased with himself. Problem solved.

Chapter 55

Nikos tired quickly. The effects of the anaesthetic and the heavy painkillers made him sleepy. His eyes become heavy and started to close. But not before he had given Christos a good description of the man who shot him and a brief description of their boat.

Christos was certain it was the Albanians, and he prayed they had not harmed the women, although he didn't mention those concerns to Nikos and the others. He wanted to talk to the rest of the crew, but felt sure they would be unable to add anything more to what they already knew. The three of them made their way back to the port where Dimitris was waiting to take them to *The Angel*.

Michalis described how he had been woken by the sound of a single gunshot, but by the time he reached the deck, the boat was speeding away. Nikos was on the floor lying in a pool of blood. At that point he had no idea that the women had been taken. The other two crew members gave a similar story. The first time they knew the women were missing was when Elias went to check on them.

Christos was frustrated. With no real clues, he was unsure of his next move. He only hoped Interpol was getting ready to move into action soon and they could bring in Officer Kallis and Tobias Panagos for questioning. That didn't help him find the two English women though.

"Shit," said Yiannis, as his phone rang. "It's Matt. What the hell do I tell him?"

"Tell him the truth," replied Costas. "He needs to know what's happened and where we are with it in case this has a bad ending."

Yiannis nodded as he accepted the call.

"Hello, Matt."

"Hi, Yiannis, just thought I'd give you a quick call to make sure the girls are OK. I've been trying to phone them, but it doesn't seem as if they've got their phones back yet. Is everything OK?"

"No, Matt, regrettably we have a situation here." Yiannis explained what happened overnight, trying to keep it as brief as possible.

"Oh my God, I'm on my way."

"No, Matt, there's no need. We have everything under control." Yiannis hoped that was true, but looking at his boss' worried face, he had his doubts.

"I'm coming, so don't try to stop me. I will be in Rhodes as soon as I can be." He ended the call.

"We now have another problem too," said Christos, who had taken a call at the same time Yiannis was talking to Matt. "The station has just taken a call from the police in the UK. It seems that Donna's husband has heard nothing from his wife for a week, and that's totally out of character. He's phoned her hotel here in Rhodes and they told him she hasn't been seen since their trip to Symi. Naturally he's extremely concerned. We need to bring him up to date but the last thing we need is him hot-footing it over here too."

"OK, I'll get the sergeant at the station to give him a call and let him know that we are investigating. I'm not sure we can put his mind at rest, especially with his wife still missing, but we do need to tell him something."

CHAPTER 55

"I think we should go to Symi," said Christos. "My gut instinct tells me that Kallis is involved in this, as is Panagos at the monastery. We'll interview them both and with a bit of luck it will rattle a few cages. Yiannis, organise a boat to take us over there as soon as possible. The sooner we get there the better our chances will be of finding the women alive."

"OK, boss, onto it."

Chapter 56

Tobias unlocked and slowly pushed open the door to the shack. He presumed the two women would be where he left them as the lock was still securely in place, but he needed to be careful in case they were waiting to ambush him.

Still in the same spot he had left them during the night, they looked tired and scared, and he was sorry about that. He wondered how the blonde had managed to get her hands in front of her. He checked the ropes, but she was still securely bound.

He opened a bottle of water and put it between her hands. Fiona drank thirstily.

"Please, could I have my hands in front of me?" asked Donna. "Otherwise I can't hold the water." Tobias thought about it but realised she was right. He knew it was risky to untie her, but if she were to eat and drink, then she needed her hands.

"OK," he said, "but no funny business."

Donna knew this might be her only chance to strike, but as soon as Tobias removed the ropes pins and needles set in as the blood started to flow. Her hands and arms became painful and the chance to attack was lost as Tobias quickly brought her arms round to the front and retied them at the wrists.

Fuck, she thought, *I've just wasted the only opportunity we might have.*

Tobias undid the second bottle of water and placed it in Donna's hands. He put a bag of bread and cheese next to each of them and then turned to leave.

"Don't go," called Fiona. "What's happening, what will happen to us next?"

"Nothing today, don't worry. I will be back tomorrow," he said, closing and locking the door behind him.

"Don't worry, my arse," said Donna. "What the hell does he think we're going to do. We've been abducted, tied up and thrown into this godforsaken excuse of a shack, with no idea of what's going to happen to us, and all he can say is don't worry. Total bloody fuckwit. And just as I was thinking there might be a softer side to him, but I'm certainly not finding it yet."

"Do you think Nikos might be dead?" asked Fiona, oblivious to her friend's outburst.

"Oh, Fiona, love, I don't know. I really hope not. He's a strong, healthy man so let's remain optimistic, eh?"

Chapter 57

Lieutenant Iraklidis and Sergeant Doukas arrived back on Symi early evening and headed straight for the police station. Yiannis had phoned ahead and was told that Kallis wouldn't be on duty until six that evening.

"OK, thank you, I'll phone him then," Yiannis replied, not wanting to alert him to their impending trip over to the island. He also phoned the monastery and was told that Tobias Panagos would be there until late that evening.

The detectives headed straight to the police station just in time to see Kallis arriving for his shift. As this was to be nothing more than an initial enquiry, they went in softly, with a friendly approach, and hoped that Kallis would trip himself up during questioning.

"Officer Kallis, I am Lieutenant Iraklidis and this is Sergeant Doukas from Rhodes police. We're hoping you can help us with one of our investigations and would just like to ask you a couple of questions."

"Yes, of course but you will have to be quick because I'm just about to go on duty," said Kallis striding into the building ahead of them.

"This won't take long," replied Christos thinking what an arrogant prick the young officer was. "We understand that two British women came on a trip to Symi from Rhodes several days ago but never made it back to Rhodes. Sergeant

Doukas made a phone call and was informed by the duty officer here that two women with matching descriptions had been detained pending further investigations over a possible murder and drug smuggling, and that the detaining officer was you. Obviously we need to investigate that further, so can you explain exactly what happened, please?"

"Certainly," said Kallis, "the two women arrived outside the police station here driving a white pickup truck with boxes of drugs in the back and a dead body. I detained both women in the cells overnight, in order that I could check their stories and get the post-mortem results from Rhodes."

"And did their stories check out?" asked Yiannis.

"Difficult to say, sir, there were no witnesses to confirm their story. No-one remembers seeing them at the monastery, but then they probably arrived with a boat full of tourists, and as you know, one tourist looks very much like another. According to the women, they needed to find a toilet and missed the boat onwards to the harbour here. Eventually they found Costas Papadopoulis at the rear of the gift shop and asked him for a lift to the port so they could catch their boat. Papadopoulis died en route, and they claimed they did not know that he was carrying drugs."

"What happened to the drugs?" asked Christos.

"I do not know. Officer Giorgiou drove the pickup truck around to the rear of the station where the body was dealt with for its onward journey to the coroner's office, and I presume he put the drugs into storage."

"OK, thank you," said Christos. "We will just need to check with Officer Giorgiou, but that can wait until tomorrow. One last thing, what happened to the two women?"

"Again, I don't know. I understand that the post-mortem results showed that Papadopoulis' death was by natural causes, a heart attack to be precise, so I presume the women were released without charge."

CHAPTER 57

"Even though there was still the matter of the drug smuggling?" asked Yiannis.

"Well, yes. After I went off duty that evening, I really had nothing further to do with the case. Officer Giorgiou must have been satisfied that there was no case to answer and released them." They had to give Kallis his due, he really was keeping his cool and had an answer for just about everything.

"Thank you very much, Officer Kallis, you've been most helpful," said Lieutenant Iraklidis, and he and Yiannis turned to leave.

"Just one thing," said Sergeant Doukas, "why haven't the records been updated on your system?"

"Oh, haven't they?" For the first time, Officer Kallis appeared a little flustered. "Well, that's down to Officer Giorgiou. If he doesn't complete the records then that's hardly any fault of mine, is it?"

"No, no of course," replied Sergeant Doukas, "I just wondered whether you could throw any light on it at all. Thank you for your time."

Christos and Yiannis left the police station.

"I don't like him," said Yiannis, "and I don't trust him one little bit. My money is on him being involved in the whole thing."

"Me neither, but we need some hard evidence against him and not just our own supposition," replied Christos. "Come on, it's getting late and we still need to interview Panagos before we call it a day."

They headed round to the harbour master's office to see if they could get a lift down to the southern end of the island. Not only did they get a lift, but the harbour master was quite chatty. In fact, he was very chatty indeed.

Chapter 58

Tobias Panagos wasn't happy to see the two detectives but knew there was nothing he could do to avoid the questioning that was about to take place.

"Mr Panagos, I'm glad we've just managed to catch you before you leave for the day. We just have a couple of questions that we need to ask but that won't take long and then you can get home to your family." Lieutenant Iraklidis was trying to be as nice as possible to put this man at ease.

"OK," said Panagos, but it was clear that he would rather be anywhere than here right now.

"Mr Panagos, did you know that Costas Papadopoulis was transporting drugs from the monastery to the main harbour?"

"No, no, I didn't."

"Does, or rather did, the white pickup truck belong to Mr Papadopoulis or is it owned by the monastery?"

"It was Costas' truck."

"What vehicle do you drive, Mr Panagos?" Yiannis slipped into the conversation.

"I have a small maroon van."

"And were you in your small maroon van in the harbour one afternoon last week?" asked Yiannis.

"No, no, I was here at the monastery all the time."

"So it wasn't you at the back of the police station transferring white boxes from Mr Papadopoulis' truck into your maroon van?" Yiannis was being persistent and Tobias was squirming.

"No, no, not me."

"Thank you," said Christos. "You have been most helpful. One last thing, where is your van now?"

"It's behind the gift shop."

"Good." Christos was still playing the friendly card, but he could see that Panagos was becoming more and more rattled. "Just wanted to make sure that it hadn't been stolen and used in a crime."

"No, no, it's been with me all the time."

"Good, good. You won't mind then if we just have a quick look on our way out, just so we can note in our report that we have seen the vehicle, and all seems in order."

Tobias led them through to the back of the gift shop. He was feeling slightly relieved that this interview was coming to a close, but he wasn't happy that they knew about his van. Thank God he had moved the boxes and stored them around the back of the shack. They should be safe there.

Chapter 59

Christos and Yiannis caught the last ferry of the day back to Rhodes. Although they were no further forward in finding the two English women, they had gleaned some useful information.

Grateful that most of the tourists had already returned to Rhodes, they found a couple of seats away from the remaining few passengers.

"OK," said Christos, "what have we got?"

"Well, Kallis gave nothing away, which is what we expected. But he did look uncomfortable when asked why the records were not up to date. Quick to pass the blame to Officer Giorgiou and not take any responsibility himself."

"Ah, but he did give something away," responded Christos. "He claimed he had no idea what had happened to the boxes with the drugs inside, presuming them to be in storage. But according to Fiona, he was at the back of the police station loading them into Panagos' maroon van. Panagos matches the description given by Fiona when she saw them both from the cell window. We now need to find the evidence. We could do with finding those boxes but they may have already left the island."

"I think that Panagos will be the easier of the two to break with some persistent questioning." Yiannis would have liked more time firing questions at him. If he had his way, he would have kept on at him until he told them where the women were. That's if he knew of course.

"Yes, you're right, Yiannis, but at the moment it's only circumstantial evidence and I don't what to scare him or Kallis off. This is much bigger than the pair of them and I will feel much happier when we have the women safe."

"OK, I understand. So do we have anything useful from the harbour master?"

"What we know is that Kallis went storming round there demanding to know the vessel identification number of the boat that picked up the two women and Spiros, even though he claims he had nothing more to do with the case after the initial detainment.

"We know that the harbour master told him the boat belonged to Vasi Thalasoss, and you can bet your life that he hot-tailed it to Rhodes to find out where he took the group. We should interview Thalasoss, but I'm pretty sure that he will confirm that he told Kallis he took the women to *The Angel*.

"What we need to know now," said Christos using his fingers to highlight his points, "is a) where the women are, b) who, and how many, are holding them, c) what the Albanians' involvement is, and d) where the boxes of drugs are and can we get fingerprints?"

"Mmm, well we've come up with a lot of theory today, but nothing that gets us any further in finding Fiona and Donna." Yiannis was feeling disappointed and didn't know what he would say to Matt when he turned up.

"Let's see what tomorrow's developments are and if we're no further forward, then we will seriously consider bringing Panagos in for further questioning, even bringing him over to Rhodes if necessary, and make him sweat a little more. I want those women back and unharmed."

Chapter 60

Wednesday

Maria was back at the hospital the following afternoon, grateful to see that Nikos was sitting up in bed and looking much better, although still a little grey.

"What's happening, Maria, are the girls back?"

"No, I'm afraid not. The police have been on board *The Angel* and taken statements from us all, but the most any of us saw was you lying on the deck and a boat speeding away. You are the only one who saw who took the ladies. It is all very distressing."

"OK, Maria. I need to get out of here. Have you brought me some fresh clothes?"

"Yes, I had a feeling that's what you would say. Here," she said, handing him a brown Louis Vuitton holdall. "I will wait outside while you get changed. Dimitri is waiting to take us back to *The Angel*."

The doctor appeared within minutes of Maria leaving Nikos alone to change clothes.

"What are you doing?"

"I'm sorry," said Nikos, pulling on a pair of jeans, "but I need to be home. My two friends are still missing, and I must do all I can to help find them."

"Mr Laskaris, you have just been shot and had major surgery. You are very lucky to be alive. Although the bullet missed all vital organs, it did damage the muscle and soft tissue. You must get plenty of rest and allow your body to mend, and I would much prefer if you did that here in this hospital where we can keep you under observation."

"Thank you, Doctor. I hear what you're saying, and I am very grateful for all that you have done for me, but I really must insist on discharging myself now."

"Very well, if I can't persuade you otherwise. I will ask the nurse to come and change the dressings and provide you with support for your arm. I will write you up a prescription for pain relief and, believe me, you will need them over the coming few weeks. Any problems at all and you must come straight back, am I making myself clear?"

"Yes, thank you," responded Nikos, unused to being treated like a naughty schoolboy.

Within the hour Nikos was ready to leave the hospital and he and Maria made their way back to the port in Lakki where Dimitri was waiting for them.

His need to get back to *The Angel* was almost overwhelming. If the police couldn't find Fiona and Donna, then he would, and he knew just the person to help him.

Chapter 61

After another night spent in the shack all Donna and Fiona had achieved was to make their wrists more painful. They had worked away at their ropes for most of the day but the bleeding was getting worse, the wrists were swelling horribly and the skin around the open sores was turning a bluish colour. It worried Donna that infection might set in.

Fiona was worried about Nikos, she feared he was dead despite Donna telling her to keep positive and send good thoughts out to him. Fiona couldn't understand why her feelings were so strong about a man she had only just met. Yes, he was good looking and a lovely man, but it was much more than that. She felt a connection on a much deeper level. She had never felt this way about a man before. Even Jeremy, when they first met, hadn't made her feel this deeply. The thought of losing it all so soon was unbearable. She had no idea where her friendship with this man was heading, probably nowhere at all, but she just wanted to spend a few more days with him.

Donna was deep in her own thoughts, terrified that she may never see Dave or her boys again. Her family was her life and not being with them was unbearable. Was this how her life was going to end? Realising she was wallowing in self-pity, she gave herself a mental kick up the arse. She simply would not accept that this was the end, she was going to fight her way out of the mess they had got themselves in, and woe betide anyone who got in her way.

"Fiona, do you want to die here at the hands of these men?"

"No," Fiona wailed, "but I don't see what we can do."

"No, I get that, but we are not giving in easily and those bastards are going to get what's coming to them."

"But how are we going to get out of these ropes? My wrists hurt so much I don't think I can keep on trying to undo them."

"No, I agree. I'm in agony too. But we've only been concentrating on getting our hands free. What if we move down to our ankles and try there?"

"What good will freeing our ankles do if our hands are still tied?" Fiona really was in a low mood and Donna didn't like it one bit. She needed to get her friend back to her usual 'can do' frame of mind.

"If our feet are free, Fiona, we can move. We can walk, we can run. We could move around and get some feeling back in our bodies. We can kick the bastards. I just think it will be better to have some part of our bodies free rather than just lying about passively waiting for them to do their worst."

"OK," replied Fiona, slowly cottoning onto the fact that any activity was better than no activity. "Let's give it a go then."

They worked on the ties binding their ankles for the rest of the morning. It was painful and caused a lot more friction with the ropes against their wrists, but the ankle bindings were not as tight, and slowly they began to loosen. It filled them with renewed hope.

That was until they heard the vehicle return.

Chapter 62

Back on the yacht and Nikos took control. He felt an overwhelming need to return to Rhodes, so had Michalis get underway as soon as possible. Now that Donna and Fiona were no longer on board, there was no need to be so cautious. He wanted to return to their permanent mooring in the harbour of the Old Town so he could be closer to the two detectives handling the case. He phoned Yiannis requesting an urgent update later that afternoon and Yiannis agreed that he and Christos would board *The Angel* soon after they docked.

His next call was to Spiros, hopeful their conversation might bring results.

"Spiros, it's Nikos."

"Nikos, it's good to hear from you. How are you, my friend?" Christos had phoned Spiros earlier to let him know that Nikos had been shot but was fine, and to give him an overall update on where they were with the case.

"Well, I survived," Nikos responded. "The bullet did a bit of damage but I'll recover. Do you have any news about the girls?"

"No, nothing yet. But to be honest, Nikos, there is nothing more I can do until those responsible for taking them are caught and charged. I know that Christos and Yiannis are working to track down their whereabouts so hopefully they will have some news soon."

"Well, there may well be something you can do, or at least something that Lucas can do. Where is he at the moment?"

"He's home right now. Why? What do you have in mind?" asked Spiros, becoming a little uneasy about what might be asked of his son.

Lucas had spent several years in the Special Operations Force but after taking a bullet during an overseas detachment a few years back, had been flown home and retired on medical grounds. But Lucas recovered well and was now picking up a lot of private work within security, protection and the odd rescue. He was as hard as they came and extremely good at what he did, but always worked with integrity. Lucas was in high demand and was a good guy to have on your side.

"I am wondering if he would be interested in a private job for me. The two women need rescuing, and Lucas is the only one I trust to get the job done. I will pay well. Would you ask him please, Spiros, and, if he is interested, please have him come on board *The Angel* this afternoon. You come too of course."

"OK," said Spiros, "I will ask him, but I need you to know that I am not totally happy with the work he does. I know he works with a good heart but it is always dangerous work. I will call you back as soon as I have his answer."

"Thank you, Spiros. I am very grateful. I wouldn't normally ask but I am very concerned for the women's safety."

Nikos ended the call just as Maria came back onto the terrace and started fussing around him. Eventually he gave in for a bit of peace and retired to his cabin for a nap. He was feeling tired and wanted to be ready for when the detectives and Lucas arrived later.

Chapter 63

"YIANNIS!" Lieutenant Iraklidis shouted from his office doorway. It was late afternoon, and he had just received the report from the Hellenic Coast Guard detailing the whereabouts of the Albanian vessel over the past six months. Christos was in a jubilant mood.

"We now have the evidence that connects the Albanians to the monastery and to Gialos in the main port," he said, waiving the piece of paper. "There is no longer any doubt in my mind that Kallis and Panagos are involved. Although we have no evidence that the Albanians abducted the women, and we don't know where they are or even if they are still alive, their vessel was last seen in Leros."

Yiannis was triumphant. It was clear from the report that the vessel had been in and out of Symi, both at the chief port at Gialos, and had also been seen entering a small cove just around the coast from the monastery. But more crucially, it had been seen entering Alinda Bay in Leros.

"Is that enough to bring Panagos in for more questioning?" asked Yiannis.

"Absolutely, and we'll definitely have more chance getting the truth out of him. Kallis will be a much tougher nut to crack. First thing in the morning we'll pick him up, so organise a boat please. If necessary we may have to bring him back here to Rhodes."

"Yes, boss," replied Yiannis. "By the way, I had a phone call from Nikos a few minutes ago. It seems he has discharged himself from the hospital in Leros and *The Angel* is now heading back to its berth here in Rhodes. He's asked if we can bring him up to speed on developments."

"OK, yes, I suppose we owe him an update, especially as he was good enough to take the two women and got himself shot for his trouble. There's not too much we can tell him at the moment, but let's just play it by ear. I think by this time tomorrow we'll know the whereabouts of the women and, hopefully, be able to secure their release."

"I'll call him and let him know. I said we would go to him on the yacht, is that OK?"

"Yes, let's. Much nicer sitting on his deck than stuck in this stuffy office."

Chapter 64

Donna and Fiona heard voices outside, but they couldn't make out what was being said. Neither could they determine how many men were talking, but they knew there was enough to cause a problem. Their ropes had loosened considerably, but still not enough to free their feet.

They didn't know what time of day it was, but by the stifling heat in the shack it must have been sometime late afternoon.

The shack door opened and Kallis appeared, silhouetted against the late afternoon sunlight streaming in. He didn't say a word, simply walked over to the girls, checked their ropes, and walked out again. Confident they were still secure he left the door open, which was a blessing as it allowed a little more air to circulate around the shack. It also allowed Fiona and Donna to hear what was being said.

"Plans have changed again and tonight a boat will come and pick up the two women plus the boxes. Make sure everything is ready down at the cove just after midnight. I want no cock-ups this time, and there is to be no trace left behind. Tobias, after you take the women to the cove you come back here and clear away everything in this shack. Set fire to it if you have to, I want nothing left behind. Do I make myself clear?" This was his last chance to dispose of the evidence, and finally he had persuaded the Albanians' boss to take care of the women. He needed it to go without a hitch.

"Yes, Yiorgos," said Tobias meekly. The Albanians simply shrugged. They couldn't give a shit about this jumped-up petty police officer and would happily take him out of the picture with a blink of an eye. But he had messed up the operation and there would be consequences if they didn't follow orders. They just had to bide their time, clear up the mess he had created, and then maybe they could clear him out of the way too and cross Symi off their list completely. It was becoming more trouble than it was worth.

Tobias busied himself unloading a few supplies from the back of his van. The Albanians had demanded food and beer and he felt the women should have something, too.

"Why are you feeding those women? It's a waste of money, they will be gone later," said Kallis.

Regardless of what Kallis said, Tobias took some food and water into the shack when his back was turned.

The two women were still sitting where he left them. They pulled at his heartstrings and he decided then and there that after all this was over he would no longer have anything to do with Kallis. He would just walk away, even if it meant leaving the island. It was one thing to pack and move boxes of drugs; he never gave a thought to the lives he may have ruined there. It was another thing seeing these two ladies being treated so badly and handed over to the Albanians. What chance would they have there? He wondered whether there was anything he could do to help that wouldn't have harsh consequences. He walked back outside, mulling it over.

"Shit, Donna," said Fiona, after Tobias had left the shack, "whatever's happening it's going to be tonight."

"Yeah, so we need to be ready. Let's hope we can get these ropes off our ankles in time. We can at least use our feet."

They heard the vehicle drive away and knew that their time was quickly running out.

Chapter 65

After giving in to Maria's fussing and retreating to his cabin for a nap, Nikos was feeling better. Once the painkillers he'd just swallowed took effect, he would be more comfortable.

Spiros and Lucas arrived on board *The Angel* late afternoon.

"Hello, Spiros," Nikos greeted his old friend with a hug. "Lucas, it's good to see you again, and thank you for agreeing to meet with me. Please, sit down. What can I get you both to drink?"

Settled with a beer each, Nikos outlined a rough plan to get the women back. But it was so full of holes that Lucas didn't think it was viable. If he were to rescue these women, then the last thing he needed was a plan devised by a man charged with emotion.

Lucas didn't pull any punches and told Nikos immediately that his idea was rubbish.

"I'm sorry, Nikos, but your plan is just not possible. I will need a lot more information before I could agree to even attempting a rescue. Where is that information likely to come from?"

"Christos Iraklidis and his sergeant will be here shortly and hopefully they will give you more details."

"I'm sorry, Nikos, I can't get involved if there if police are investigating." said Lucas holding his hands up and backing away from the whole operation.

"Please, Lucas, I'm begging you, please get the ladies back."

"Lucas," began Spiros, "I know you work below the radar, son, but Christos is also a friend of mine, and I promise you he will not ask too many questions. His eye is on the bigger picture. He is working with Interpol to smash a major drug smuggling ring, of which this is just a small part. Please, just listen to what he has to say and then make your decision based on that. This could be mutually beneficial to everyone."

"OK, Papa, for you I will listen, but I won't make any promises until I am satisfied that there is some hope of success."

"Thank you," said Nikos. "I understand, but I am desperate to secure the ladies' release."

Spiros looked at Nikos questioningly, wondering why he was so anxious for two women he had only just met. There was a lot more to this than Nikos was saying.

Thirty minutes later the detectives boarded the yacht. After accepting a cold beer they got down to business.

"Before we start, let me give you these. They are the ladies' possessions we picked up from Symi," Christos pushed a package across the table towards Nikos.

"OK, now first things first," Christos said, "there's been a development." He looked at Lucas as he continued. "We received a tip-off just before we left the station. The ladies are being held on Symi and will be picked up sometime after midnight by the Albanians."

"Do you know the exact location?" asked Lucas.

Yiannis unfurled a detailed map of the island and lay it across the table.

CHAPTER 65

"The pickup point is here," he said, pointing to a small cove a little way round from the monastery. "At the moment the women are being held in some sort of shack which we believe to be here, but we can't be absolutely certain. They will be moved to the cove around midnight, but again, we can't be sure. It is very secluded in this area so there's no chance of being seen."

"OK," said Lucas, looking happier. "It will be far easier to attempt the rescue from the shack. The cove is too open. Do we know how many people are involved?"

"No," replied Yiannis, "all we know is that Kallis and Tobias Panagos are the two involved on Symi but we don't know how many Albanians are on the island. Kallis won't be guarding them. He doesn't like to do too much work, and I wouldn't trust Panagos to guard a dog. My guess is there are a couple of Albanians. How many will come in tonight for the pickup is anyone's guess, but I wouldn't have thought they would need too many for a couple of women."

Lucas went quiet for a while, considering his best options. Christos updated Nikos and Spiros on their findings over the past couple of days.

"This is what I propose my plan of action to be," said Lucas, "but to be honest I don't care if you have objections, it is still my plan of action."

The group of men listened to Lucas' plan. He first needed to find a colleague available to work with him at short notice and that would come at a price. Nikos nodded in total agreement. He was just happy that Lucas knew exactly what he was doing, and he trusted him to get the job done. He also wanted assurance that the police would have no interest in him once the mission had been completed, whether successful or not.

"Agreed, and thank you, Lucas," said Christos. "We will leave you to rescue the ladies from the shack but will have a backup team ready to go in and pick up the Albanians as soon as you are clear. I will have another, larger, team in place at the cove to pick up the incoming Albanians and hopefully Kallis and Panagos. I will contact Interpol and check on the status of the overall operation. Keep me informed, Lucas, I must know what's going on. We should go now and make our own preparations, but my teams will be in position before midnight."

Christos and Yiannis said their farewells and disembarked.

"Where do you want me to take the women once we have them?" Lucas asked Nikos.

"Bring them here. I will ensure their safety until the whole operation has been concluded."

"OK. I must go now and make my own arrangements. Hopefully, all will go well and I will see you later, Nikos."

Lucas and Spiros left *The Angel* and Nikos retired to his cabin to rest. There was nothing more he could do, although he would have dearly loved to have gone on the rescue mission. But he had to trust that Lucas had everything under control and would bring Fiona and Donna back safely.

Chapter 66

Daylight was beginning to fade rapidly. After working on their ankle bindings all afternoon they finally loosened them enough to slip their feet through the loops. Movement to their legs was agony as the blood began to circulate. Half an hour later they had some feeling back and could walk around the shack, albeit shakily.

Although not hungry they ate the food and drunk the water Tobias left, purely to keep their energy levels up. They kept moving. They wanted to regain as much strength in their legs as possible if they were to stand half a chance of making their escape later. Donna still didn't know how that might happen, but she was determined to cause as much fuss as possible and make it as difficult as she could for their captors.

Voices outside the shack were getting louder and, alongside the bouts of raucous laughter, it masked any noise the girls were making. It sounded like two people, but they couldn't be certain. Two people were better than four to deal with, thought Fiona and suggested they should try to get out of the shack sooner rather than later. The only problem was with their hands still tied, any movement in their arms was excruciating.

Donna moved around the inside walls, checking to see whether there were any weakened pieces of wood that they might be able to prise off. If they could make a big enough hole to climb through, they could make their escape.

She found an area in a corner, quite low to the ground, where the wood was rotting and weak. Donna pulled, but it hurt. She beckoned Fiona over.

"Look," she whispered, although there wasn't much chance of them being overheard. "If we can pull those couple of slats off, I reckon we could squeeze through the hole and escape, but it's hurting my wrists so much that we should probably take it in turns. What do you reckon?"

"Hell yes," replied Fiona, "and the quicker we get out the better. I've no idea where we are, so we might have to hide until it gets light, but it will be better than just sitting here and accepting our fate. Let me have a go."

Renewed with hope, the girls took turns in loosening the slats. Slowly they made progress, but it was a race against time.

Chapter 67

Christos made the call to Pierre Bernier at Interpol and explained the situation on Symi. Bernier confirmed all teams would be in place by midnight and he would give the order to go at precisely 01:00 hours.

Christos organised a team to be in place at the cove by eleven-thirty. He wasn't expecting any activity until the early hours of the morning, but he didn't want to miss a boat coming in. He had no idea how large the vessel might be, or how many men were involved, but he reasoned it couldn't be too big if it was to pull alongside the small wooden jetty.

He had liaised with Lucas over timings. They would make their move at the shack at eleven-fifteen, which should give them plenty of time to rescue the women and make their escape. Christos didn't like involving non-police personnel in his operations, and especially ex-military who operated by instinct rather than rules, but he had the safety of two women, and British women at that, in his hands, so he had relented. He wouldn't mention Lucas' involvement unless he absolutely had to.

Running on adrenaline, Yiannis was eager to get going. They didn't know where Kallis and Panagos would be, but logic told them that the cove was the most sensible option. Kallis would want to know that the women had gone, and he wouldn't trust Panagos to act on his own. Christos and

Yiannis planned to be at the cove and had officers and vehicles standing by.

It was time to leave, and Christos hoped and prayed that all would go according to plan.

Chapter 68

All teams were in position well before midnight. Eight armed officers were spread out and well-hidden around the cove, with a further officer and vehicle hidden about half a mile back along the gravel track, ready to drive down to the cove when the order was given. All was quiet. No boats could be seen or heard, but they knew they were coming.

They waited.

Iraklidis and Doukas had arrived earlier along the western side of Symi by helicopter. Although it was rough terrain, the pilot found a clearing big enough to land and remained in position, just in case he was needed. Silently they made their way down to the beach.

They waited.

A further four armed officers were spread roughly two hundred yards back from the shack, two at the front and two at the rear. Their approach had been silent, their vehicle left half a mile away. Their orders were to wait until they had received confirmation that the women were safe, and then go in and pick up the Albanians.

They waited.

Lucas and his colleague, Steve, were silent in their approach. No-one, not even the officers, heard them coming. Dressed head to toe in black, they carried no firearms, just a knife each. Slowly and silently, they made their way to the rear of the shack, searching for their best point of entry. It didn't take them long to find it.

Low to the ground on the near corner was an opening with a woman's head poking through it.

Chapter 69

The girls had worked hard and, although suffering for their efforts, had made a hole big enough to squeeze through. It was pitch black outside. Even the moon seemed to have taken cover. They had a rough plan to squeeze through the hole and make their way towards whatever landmark they might see. If they could see nothing, then they would get as far away from the shack as they could and wait for daylight.

After a few deep breaths they were finally ready. Donna went first. She lay on her front on the floor and used her feet and elbows to push herself forward towards the gap. She grunted in pain, her arms and hands hurt like hell but she kept shuffling onwards. Slowly she reached the hole. Another deep breath as she poked her head through.

Immediately she felt a hand clamp across her mouth.

Fuck, bugger, bum, shit, she thought, *they've found us already.*

A pair of eyes stared at her through a black balaclava. A shake of the head and a finger to the lips silenced her, and slowly the hand was released.

"Ssshhh, you're safe," the voice whispered, as hands helped pull her through the hole.

"Fiona," she whispered, and pointed back through the hole.

The head nodded. "Get her," it said.

Donna wasn't sure if they were safe or not, but she had no choice now but to trust her gut instinct. There were two of them and logic told her they wouldn't be dressed in black from head to toe and silent if they were working with the Albanians, who were still kicking up a hell of a racket at the front of the shack.

Donna put her bound hands back through the hole and beckoned Fiona out. As Fiona's head came through the hole, the same hand clamped over her mouth, but Fiona was quick and squirmed backwards into the shack and the hand lost contact.

"No you bloody don't," said Fiona. "I'm not making it that easy for you."

"Fuck," said Donna. She got down on the ground again and put her head back through the hole. The movement was killing her wrists and she wished that for once Fiona would just keep to the sodding plan.

"Fiona," she whispered, "it's alright we're being rescued. Come out. Hurry up and keep quiet."

Fiona looked at Donna, unsure whether she was telling the truth or being coerced into getting Fiona out of the shack.

"Will you just bloody well get out here," Donna's whispers were getting louder as she became more and more exasperated with Fiona's reluctance.

"Fiona, move your bloody arse now before you get us all killed."

Slowly Fiona put her head back through the hole and stared wide-eyed at the two men in black.

Once through, the men took out their knives and cut their wrist bindings. The pain was agonising as the blood began circulating. It was all they could do to stop crying out. Slowly the pain eased as feeling gradually came back into their hands.

"Come," whispered Lucas, "we need to get out of here as quickly as possible." Slowly they made their way across the rough terrain and away from the shack. It was hard going. Helped by the two men they made their way in silence.

"Nikos?" asked Fiona finally, dreading the reply. She didn't know who these men were or where they were taking them, but she needed to know about Nikos. Lucas stopped for a moment, satisfied they were out of earshot but still eager to get the women back to the yacht.

"Fiona, Donna, I am Lucas Galanis, son of Spiros, your solicitor. You're both safe now. Nikos is safe and we are taking you back to *The Angel*. Now we must keep moving. We have a dinghy moored about half a mile away and the sooner we get away from here the better."

Fiona started to shake and cry.

"It's OK now, you are both safe," said Steve in a quiet and soothing voice as he popped an arm around Fiona's shoulder. That was her undoing. Relief flooded through her as she collapsed against him and sobbed her heart out. Donna moved in close and put her arms around her dearest friend, holding her while she let it all out. Donna was feeling fragile and emotional too, but she would hold on until she was alone. She knew once she opened the floodgates it would take a while to stop.

Slowly, they made their way to the dinghy. Steve jumped in as Lucas picked Donna up in his arms and handed her across. Once she was settled, they did the same with Fiona, untied the holding ropes, and pushed away from the shore.

Lucas sent a message to Team Two, confirming that the women were safely away from the island. He messaged Christos with the same confirmation and finally sent a third message to Nikos saying 'mission successful, on our way back'.

Chapter 70

As soon as Lucas had the dinghy safely away from the shore and out of earshot, he dropped the oars and triggered the outboard motor. They made good progress.

Hearing the rumble of the engine Nikos made his way down to the lower deck and watched as the dinghy approached. He found it impossible to sleep whilst he waited, despite Maria's nagging. There would be time to sleep later but for now he needed to see Fiona and make sure they were both OK after their ordeal. He also needed to apologise. He felt guilty for not keeping them safe, and he would not let that happen again.

The engine quietened as Lucas brought the dinghy in close to the rear of the yacht. Steve jumped aboard and secured it, and then turned to help the girls. Fiona was already standing and grabbing the side rail, eager to get to Nikos.

"Oh Nikos, I'm so sorry." Fiona could feel the tears gather as she took his outstretched hand and stepped onto *The Angel*.

"No, no, my love, it is I who should be sorry. I failed to keep you both safe."

"No, it's our fault. We should never have come on board and involved you in all of this. They could have killed you."

"But we're all safe now," Donna felt she needed to put an end to these self-recriminations before it all got out of hand,

"and it will only get better." She climbed from the dinghy and moved closer to Nikos and, greeting him with a kiss on both cheeks, was pleased to see that he wasn't looking too bad.

Still in some discomfort, he gently returned both of their hugs, lingering much longer with Fiona, welcoming them back on board. They moved upstairs to the indoor lounge where Maria was busying herself with hot drinks.

"It all went smoothly," Lucas told Nikos as they moved a little distance away from the others. "No casualties on our part. Two Albanians were guarding the women at the front of the shack. Fortunately for us they had drunk a little too much alcohol. We took the girls out from the rear of the shack, although they already had their own escape in progress by the time we arrived. We made our way silently back to the dinghy. The police know we have the women and as soon as we were safely away from the island they moved in to pick up the Albanians."

"Thank you very much, Lucas, I am most grateful and I will transfer your payment immediately."

"Thank you. It was my pleasure to help and if I can be of any further assistance, then please ask. One small thing, you may need to get some medical help for the ladies' wrists. They were bound pretty tightly and their struggling to free themselves has resulted in considerable injury."

"First thing in the morning I will bring a doctor on board," replied Nikos. "We will have a catch-up with Christos and Yiannis tomorrow, and your father will be present. Please join us too."

"Thank you, but no thank you," replied Lucas. "We've completed our work with no consequence, so the police won't want anything further from us. However, we will remain close and keep an eye on *The Angel* to ensure everyone's safety until we hear from either Christos or Yiannis. If you have any concerns at all, then please call me. We will be here in seconds." Lucas and Steve said their farewells amid more hugs and kisses from the girls and got back into their dinghy.

CHAPTER 70

Maria said goodnight too, warning them not to stay up too much longer, as they all needed their rest. Nikos, Fiona and Donna settled back down. Pumped with adrenaline they knew sleep would be impossible.

"First of all, Donna, your husband is extremely concerned about you and has contacted the police in the UK. Rhodes police have told him that they are investigating but have not told him that you had been abducted. I think you need to phone him immediately and put the poor man's mind at rest. The police collected your belongings from Symi and brought them here. I took the liberty of charging both your phones so they are ready to use."

"Thank you," Donna took the phone and moved to the far end of the room. It was the early hours of the morning back home but she knew Dave would not be sleeping. She dialled their home number and the phoned was answered immediately.

"Dave, it's me."

"Oh thank God, where have you been, what happened?" Donna could hear his voice break, she was sure there was tears.

"I'm so sorry, darling, it's a very long and complicated story which I will tell you all about when I get home. But we're both safe and well so I can put your mind totally at rest."

"Sweetheart, I have been so worried about you and nobody could tell me what was happening. I don't know what I would have done if I had lost you."

"Well you haven't, I'm absolutely fine and looking forward to getting home and seeing you. I love you, Dave."

"I love you too, darling, please don't ever put me through that again will you?"

"No, I promise I will call you every day from now on. I've got to go, babe, but sleep well and I promise I will phone tomorrow morning."

"Promise?"

Donna laughed, "Yes, darling, I promise. I love you."

"I love you too."

Donna ended the call and went back to the other two.

"Is he OK?" asked Fiona.

"He is now. Did you call Jeremy?"

"No, I didn't. If he's worried he can call me but somehow I don't think he will be concerned. There are no voicemail messages from him, just a few from Dave. That speaks volumes doesn't it?" Donna tended to agree with her.

"Nikos, now tell us what happened here after they took us," Donna said.

Nikos gave them an outline of what happened and how he returned to *The Angel* the following day. He didn't mention that it was against his doctor's advice. He told them how Lucas had been willing to rescue them and bring them back safely. Tomorrow they would have an update from Christos and see where they go from there.

He looked across at Donna and could see her eyes dropping.

"Right," he said, "off to bed for us all. Tomorrow we can talk more, but for now I think we all need to sleep. Fiona, Donna, please rest assured that you will be safe. Apart from Lucas and Steve, I have people keeping watch until we know that the police have locked those men up."

They made their way to their cabins and, after a quick shower, both Donna and Fiona fell into their beds.

"Why do we always end up in some kind of skulduggery when we're together?" asked Donna, as they were settling down to sleep.

"God knows, but it always happens to us, doesn't it? Perhaps we have a big sign saying 'Trouble Welcome Here' over our heads."

CHAPTER 70

"Mmm," Donna laughed, "I think this is the worse yet though."

"Yup, we've never been abducted off a multi-million pound yacht before!"

But there was no reply. Donna had already drifted off into a deep sleep.

CHAPTER 71

As soon as the message came through that the two women were safe, Team Two moved in towards the shack. Keeping low to the ground and silent, they moved swiftly. The two Albanians had no idea they were coming.

Two officers moved from the rear of the shack and joined their two colleagues at the front and sides. Still the Albanians heard nothing. Swigging beer from the bottle, the noise from their laughter drowned out the approach of Team Two. On the count of three all four officers moved in and the Albanians were taken with hardly a struggle. The whole operation was quick and simple.

Handcuffed and bundled into the back of the waiting police van, the pair were driven back to the station in the main town to be cautioned and booked. Placed in a cell overnight both would be formally charged the following day.

Down at the cove Kallis was the first to arrive. Killing the engine he left the headlights switched on, illuminating the area. With the flick of a lighter he lit a cigarette from its flame and inhaled deeply. Leaning back against the car enjoying his smoke, he waited for Tobias to arrive. He was confident that this time his plan would succeed. He heard the boat pulling alongside the wooden jetty long before he saw anything. He watched two men slowly walking up the beach towards him, a third securing the boat to the mooring post.

A vehicle approached. Kallis moved away from his car and ground his cigarette out under foot. *Perfect timing*, he thought. The pickup came to a stop just a few yards away and Tobias slowly got out.

"Tobias," said Kallis, "you won't regret joining me in this mission, and your safety is now assured. Right, let's get these two out of the pickup."

"Yiorgos, there has been a ..." began Tobias as Kallis moved towards the back of the truck.

All hell suddenly broke loose.

"Freeze, police. Drop you weapons and hands in the air." The team sprang into action from either side of the cove whilst Christos and Yiannis brought up the rear. All weapons were trained on Kallis and the three men from the vessel. Headlights from the police vehicles suddenly illuminated the area as they crept forward down to the beach. There was nowhere to run.

"You bastard," said Kallis, looking directly at Tobias. "You set me up. You will pay for this."

Kallis and the Albanians were patted down and handcuffed. Christos placed them under formal arrest and cautioned him. "Take them away," he said to his team.

Christos moved to Tobias, cautioned him but did not cuff him, and he was led away to another waiting police car.

"Thank you," murmured Lieutenant Iraklidis as he passed by.

Chapter 72

Thursday

It was mid-morning before they both woke. Fiona was the first to get out of bed, eager to check on Nikos. As she came out of the bathroom, Donna was up and ready to take her place.

Morning, sugar, how you feeling?"

"I'm OK," replied Fiona. "My wrists are so painful though and stung like hell in the shower. How about you?"

"About the same," replied Donna. "I'll get ready then I suggest we find Maria and get her to put some clean dressings on our wounds. We can also get some painkillers from her."

They found Maria on the middle deck, waiting for them. Nikos was sitting at one end of the table where a medical kit lay open and a man was examining his chest wound.

Maria came towards them, arms open wide, and gave each a hug and kiss on both cheeks. Donna welled up and she felt the tears threaten to spill over. Just a week ago she had never met these people and now they were like family.

"Please come, sit down. This is Nikos' doctor. He comes to check Nikos' wound and will check your wrists whilst he is here." Then you will eat." Maria ushered them into chairs and brought them each a glass of freshly squeezed orange juice.

With Nikos' wound covered with a fresh dressing, the doctor pronounced that it was healing nicely and he had no concerns, although Nikos still needed to take things easy. He moved across and looked at the girls' wrists. Applying some antiseptic solution, which stung and made them wince, he covered them with clean bandages. Concerned about infection, he prescribed a course of antibiotics before he left the yacht, declaring he would be back the following day and advised them all to try to keep out of trouble.

Elias, the chef and also Maria's husband, brought them some eggs and bacon, toast and coffee. He was planning a special dinner for them later, so decided a simple brunch would suffice. They had hardly eaten in the last twenty-four hours so needed something to boost their energy.

Once finished, Maria cleared away the breakfast dishes. "Right," she pointed at Nikos, "he must have plenty of rest and take things easy for a while, he needs to regain his strength." Although Maria didn't look at anyone, Fiona got the distinct impression it was aimed at her. Bloody hell, Maria didn't miss a thing. She was like an old mother hen where Nikos was concerned.

CHAPTER 73

The girls were on the upper deck, soaking up the sun and topping up their tans. It felt so good just to relax, hoping that the worst was over and they could continue to enjoy their holiday.

"Can you believe everything that's happened to us, Don?" Fiona was mulling over events of the past week and thinking about the rollercoaster of emotions they had both been through.

"No, it's like something from a film, isn't it?"

"Yes, it is. It would make a great story for the Ladies Lunch Club when I get back. That would certainly stop the lot of them burbling on about sod all."

"Bloody hell, Fi, you can't be seriously considering going back to that, surely?"

"Well, what else am I going to do? The days drag until Jeremy gets home in the evening, and often that's not till late. Anyway, I doubt he'll be speaking much when I get back. He'll want to punish me for going on holiday against his wishes."

"That man needs a serious talking to. Why don't I come and stay for a few days and set him straight?"

"No, no, please don't do that, it will only make things worse." Fiona knew that any interference from Donna, although she meant well, would set Jeremy off and she'd never hear the end of it. The only way to placate him was to totally agree with everything he said and admit that she was wrong to go away and leave him.

"Well, I think you're bloody bonkers to put up with him. He wouldn't have lasted five minutes married to me."

"I know. But we're both different characters, Donna, you and I see things differently. That's what makes our friendship so special."

Donna was gazing at the surrounding boats in the harbour, mulling over her friend's marriage and trying to understand why she put up with so much crap from a pig of a man that she wasn't in love with. She deserved much better. She deserved Nikos.

Suddenly, she sat upright and gasped.

"Oh my God, Fi! Look, isn't that the man from Paris? The one I saw in Leros the other day?"

"Don't be daft, it couldn't possibly be."

"It bloody well is. I swear it is. Look."

"Where?"

"There, on that boat just pulling out of its mooring." Fiona glanced across to where she was pointing.

"No, can't be. Impossible."

"It is, I'm telling you it's him." Donna stood and moved over to the railing for a closer view. "Yes, it definitely is him, come and look."

Fiona got up and stood next to Donna at the railing, both staring at the boat slowly moving by them.

"That's not him, Don, he's a young man. Our man would be thirty years older by now."

CHAPTER 73

"I'm telling you, Fiona, that's him. Look again."

Donna was getting exasperated. She knew beyond any doubt that the man she was looking at was the man who had been following them around Paris over thirty years ago. Gut feeling told her she was right, but convincing Fiona when she was being so bloody logical was difficult. Fiona stared at the boat and her jaw dropped.

"Jeez, Don, how can that be possible? No, can't be, it's just coincidence surely. He hasn't aged a bit."

"I know, and he's wearing the same clothes too."

"Quick, get your phone and take a couple of photos."

Donna ran back to her sunlounger and retrieved her phone from underneath. Moving quickly back to the railing, she opened the camera and started clicking away.

"At least we'll have a couple of photos to remember him by this time," she said.

And then, just as they did in Paris all those years ago, they slid into a bubble as time stood still. Only Donna, Fiona and the man existed, just for a brief moment in time. As the boat passed by, the man looked up at them, smiled and gave a thumbs-up sign, exactly as he had in Paris all those years ago.

Chapter 74

Later that afternoon, Christos and Yiannis walked along the jetty and asked permission to come on board.

Nikos and the girls had taken brief naps after lunch and were feeling refreshed once again. They'd been lounging on the deck in the shade and enjoying the peace and quiet. Donna hoped that Christos would have some good news and that everyone had been arrested and locked up. They needed to feel safe so they could enjoy the rest of their holiday; they didn't have much of it left after all the shenanigans they had managed to get themselves involved in.

"Please come on board," called Nikos, smiling, as they all made their way across to the comfy seating area. Five minutes later, Spiros joined them and Maria arrived with tall glasses of homemade lemonade.

"Ladies, it's good to see you again. How are you both?" Spiros kissed both girls on the cheeks, genuinely pleased that they were safe and unharmed.

"We're both fine now, thank you, Spiros," replied Donna.

"We're all delighted that you are now safe," said Yiannis.

Christos nodded in agreement. "OK," he began, pulling a small notebook from his pocket, "this is what we have so far. Kallis, Tobias Panagos and five Albanian men were all taken into custody last night, or I should say the early hours of this morning, and have now been transferred here to Rhodes. Kallis is professing his innocence, but I think we will have enough evidence to formally charge him with colluding in abduction with intent to murder, and involvement in a global drug-smuggling ring."

"We found the boxes of drugs that Papadopoulis was taking to the port. They were behind the shack where you were both being held," added Yiannis, looking over at Fiona and Donna. "We have fingerprinted all suspects and we're pretty confident that we will find their prints all over the consignment of drugs."

"At the same time Interpol launched Operation Trapdoor involving officers across ten different countries from Latin America and Europe. They have since smashed a major international drug-smuggling operation. We can link the five Albanians we picked up this morning to that drug-smuggling ring and they will now stand trial in Athens. We will additionally charge two of them with your abduction and one with the attempted murder of you, Nikos.

"Which only leaves Panagos, and whilst he will certainly receive a prison sentence for his part in the scheme, it is likely that the judge will deal with him a little leniently as it was he who gave us the tip-off we needed to save your lives. He has also given us the information needed to charge Kallis."

"You see," declared Donna, "I always had a feeling about that guy, there was a softer side to him."

"Yes," replied Yiannis, "we know Kallis had quite a hold over him but when it came to, er, disposing of you two, he just couldn't do it."

"Thank God for that," said Fiona, "or we could be dead by now."

"I would never have let that happen," Nikos said softly, picking up Fiona's hand. "I got Lucas involved as soon as I could, and he's the best there is. I'm so grateful to your wonderful son, Spiros."

CHAPTER 74

Spiros was proud of his boy and even more grateful that he rescued the two ladies without resorting to the use of violence, although he knew full well that he would have used force if he needed to.

"It seems highly likely that Christos will have enough evidence to secure a conviction on Kallis without you two needing to testify," said Spiros, but we should err on the side of caution and just wait for the fingerprint testing to come back."

"They should be back later today," replied Yiannis, "and then we will let you all know."

"Good, good," said Spiros, "so all being well you two ladies will be free to go back home to the UK within the next day or so."

"The initial hearing will take place in Rhodes," Christos chipped in, "but because it involves a serving police officer, they may well take it to Athens. But that really is all I can tell you at the moment."

"Phew!" said Donna. "I take it this will not happen soon then?"

"No," replied Yiannis, "it will take time to organise the trial and here we work on Greek time, which I understand is slower to your English time." Donna and Fiona laughed.

"Yiannis and I need to return to the station now," said Christos, "but as soon as we have more news one of us will let you know."

Chapter 75

"Nikos, I don't think we can ever repay you for your kindness, not only welcoming us on board *The Angel* but also for coming to our rescue when we needed it the most. I will be eternally grateful to you," said Donna after everyone had left the yacht.

"It was the very least I could do," replied Nikos. "Spiros is one of my oldest friends, and when a friend needs help, then you step in, no?"

"Yes, exactly that," she replied, "but getting yourself shot in the bargain is going above and beyond. As soon as Christos has everything confirmed, we'll go back to the hotel and get out of your way."

"No, no," said Nikos. "No, please, you must stay here for the rest of your holiday. We can collect your luggage from the hotel and then we can simply cruise the Greek islands. Please, Donna, both of you stay on my yacht and allow me to enjoy your company."

Fiona moved closer to Donna and pinched her on the backside. Although it didn't hurt at all, Donna realised that this was a warning that she needed to come up with the right answer.

"Well, if you put it like that, how could I possibly refuse," Donna replied as a big smile broke out across her face.

"Thanks, Donna," said Fiona, as she moved closer to her friend and embraced her in a big hug.

"What for?"

"For agreeing to stay on the yacht until we go home."

"Hey, it's for my benefit too, you know," replied Donna slipping an arm around her friend. "I can't think of anywhere I would rather be than here, on board a luxury yacht with sunshine, great food, plenty of wine, and my bestie. Having Dave here would be a bonus but hey, let's make the most of this, kid."

Chapter 76

As the three gathered for pre-dinner drinks on the middle deck, it surprised them to see Dimitri leave the yacht and hot-foot it along the jetty.

"Elias has probably forgotten something he needs for tonight's dinner so he's sent Dimitri off to get it," said Nikos, looking much refreshed after a quick nap when everyone had left *The Angel*. "Are you two girls staying with your usual gin and tonic, or would you like something different this evening?"

"Actually, Nikos, I think I would like an Ouzo," said Donna.

"Of course, and a great choice. Same for you too, Fiona?"

"No, thank you, I'm not a lover of the aniseed flavour, but I could murder a Bacardi and Coke."

"Coming right up. I'm sure pouring drinks is one thing I can still do."

They sat sipping their drinks and chatting. Fiona was determined to keep the conversation light, but she knew eventually Nikos would ask what happened to them after they had been taken off the yacht. The sound of Dimitris returning saved her from answering questions. A moment later and they heard two sets of footsteps coming up to the middle deck and there stood Matt.

"Matt!" shouted Donna and Fiona together and ran towards him. Matt encircled them both and the three stood in a tight hug for what seemed ages. Finally, he loosened his grip and stepped back, holding them at arm's length. He looked at them both, his eyes travelling up and down their bodies.

"Well, you both look as stunning as ever, but what's with the bandaged wrists?"

"Oh, we'll tell you about all that later, but come and say hello to Nikos. He's got a wound of his own to show."

Matt moved across to greet Nikos. Surprised, but delighted that they were all together again, they settled themselves back down and Nikos poured more drinks.

"Matt, when did you get here? In fact, why are you here?" Donna asked.

"I've been calling your mobiles but no answer, so I phoned Yiannis just to make sure you were both OK. He told me someone had abducted you, so I grabbed the first flight I could and arrived this afternoon. I couldn't believe it. I was terrified for you both. Yiannis called me earlier to say you were both safe and back on board so I called Nikos and asked if I could come this evening to see for myself that you were both OK."

"How long can you stay?" Donna asked.

"I've taken a week off work," he replied. "I will stay in Rhodes and I'd like to come back with you two. The airline have agreed to that, but it's whether you want me to hang around."

"Of course we do," Fiona couldn't think of anything nicer than getting to know their new best friend a little more.

"Matt, you must stay here on *The Angel*," said Nikos. "Together we can all relax and enjoy one another's company and we can recuperate at our leisure."

Maria set down a large tray on the low table in front of them. It was a typical Greek meze with a variety of fresh foods, and enough to feed an army.

CHAPTER 76

"The main course will be about half an hour, is that OK?" she asked Nikos.

"That's perfect, Maria, thank you."

Both Fiona and Donna still felt ravenous after days of not eating properly and constantly nibbled away at the food. Even Nikos found his appetite returning, especially now everyone was safe and they were together again. They were surprised when, a short time later, Christos and Yiannis reappeared.

"Christos, Yiannis, please do come aboard," called Nikos from the deck. They came up the stairs and joined them. "What can I get you both to drink?"

"A beer would be perfect, thank you," replied Christos. He realised he was pushing his luck by not going straight home, but they had just completed a tough case and secured the release of the two English women unharmed. It was only natural that he wanted to celebrate the successful outcome with friends.

"I'll have the same," said Yiannis, as he sat down. "Hello, Matt, it's nice to see you again. Demetrios not with you this evening?"

"No, not this evening. He has a stopover somewhere but should be back tomorrow."

"OK," said Christos, as soon as he'd taken his first swig of beer, "we have the fingerprint results back and they show positive for Kallis. His prints are not only on the outside of the boxes, but some were found inside as well. Panagos' prints were everywhere. This afternoon we have charged both with collusion in abduction and attempted murder and involvement in an international drug-smuggling ring. They are facing a very long prison sentence.

"The good news for you, ladies, is that we have more than enough evidence, so you won't be asked to testify. Your ordeal is truly over. One thing, however, Fiona, you may need to confirm in court that it was Panagos you saw moving the boxes with Kallis at the back of the police station in Symi. If that is necessary we will try to do it via satellite link to save you having to travel back." Lieutenant Christos Iraklidis was extremely happy with the outcome.

"Oh, I have no problem with coming back," said Fiona, glancing across at Nikos.

"Is now OK for dinner?" Maria asked, as she cleared away the meze.

"Yes, I think so," Nikos replied. "I think we can put all the serious business behind us now and enjoy our evening together. Gentlemen, please stay and join us for dinner."

"Thank you for the offer," said Christos, "but I really need to get home. My wife will not be pleased if I'm too late back, she has a list of tasks for me this evening. But Yiannis, please stay and enjoy your evening and I will see you in the morning."

"Thank you," said Yiannis, "I would love to join you for dinner, and I'll see you tomorrow, boss."

Chapter 77

"Donna, what do you think that man is all about?" asked Fiona, as they were getting ready for bed.

"What man?"

"The one we saw in Paris and who turned up in the harbour today. And now I'm more convinced it was him you saw in Leros too."

"Oh him. I'm absolutely certain it's the same man, but I'm not sure why he's here. I mean, we've not seen him for what, twenty-five years or so and then he turns up today looking the same as he did when we last saw him."

"Mmm, so strange."

"When we first saw him in Paris, you couldn't see him for ages after I did, yet today you saw him immediately. I don't understand that." Donna was puzzled and didn't have a feasible explanation.

"It seemed as if he knew us straight away because he gave us the thumbs-up, just like he did all those years ago." Fiona's logical mind was going into overdrive, desperately trying to find the most feasible explanation to what was a most bizarre event.

"Perhaps it's just a coincidence," suggested Donna, who was also at a complete loss to find a logical explanation.

"Did you tell anyone about him when we got back from Paris?"

"Oh Donna, I really can't remember, it was so long ago. I might have told Mum and Dad but I'm not sure whether I did really. What about you?"

"Same here, once we got home I kind of put him out of my mind. I thought about him from time to time over the years, but not too deeply. But now I'm thinking about it again, it does seem kind of odd that he turned up all over Paris, wouldn't talk to us, you couldn't see him for a long time, and he disappeared when I went to ask him why he was following us. Really bizarre."

"And how did he know where we were going to be? He was just there, wherever we went he turned up. It was like he was listening to us, hearing our conversations, but I know that wasn't possible." The more Fiona tried to think of a logical answer, the more it eluded her. Perhaps there just wasn't one.

"Yes, and then he turned up at the airport and waved us off, but only after our flight had been changed. It was as if he knew and was happy about it. What was that all about?"

"Heaven knows."

They went quiet as they got into bed, both lost in their own minds with thoughts of the man going round and round in their heads. Sleep was a long way off for them both.

"Unless ..." started Donna, but she left the sentence unfinished.

"Unless what?"

"No, that's just stupid."

"Just say it, Donna, however stupid it sounds."

"Well, unless he was there to look after us. I mean, he turned up in all the places we went, made sure we saw him but then disappeared. Then he turned up at the airport and for whatever reason we had to change flights. He smiled and gave us the thumbs-up, as if he knew we had to change to another flight, and then we heard that our original flight crashed and everyone on board died."

"Yes, I agree it's a bloody big coincidence, but I think that's all it is, Donna. I mean, how could he possibly have got our flights changed?"

"He could if he's some sort of guardian angel."

"Now you're just being bloody ridiculous."

"Well just think about it for a minute. The first time we saw him was in Paris, we were supposed to get on a flight that crashed, killing everyone on board. We didn't get on that flight, for whatever reason, and he turned up and gave a thumbs-up. He knew that we would be OK. With me so far?"

"Yes, of course I am."

"Right, then he turns up again today after twenty-five years or so and gives the exact same smile and thumbs-up. He knows we'll be OK now, after we've been abducted and God knows what."

"Well I see what you're saying, but a guardian angel? Come on, Donna, I think that's just one step too far."

"No, it isn't. Fiona, I've seen too many people die and too many strange things happening when they do, so I know that there's more to life than just this. I know that we go onwards after our physical bodies die."

"Really?"

"Yes, really. So until you can come up with a much more logical explanation of who this man is, I think I'm going to believe he's our guardian angel and he's keeping us safe."

"So if he's keeping us safe how come we got abducted? Explain that one."

"Well, perhaps he can't stop everything from happening, but we didn't end up dead, did we?"

"Oh Donna, it all sounds a bit fanciful to me. I'm not really sure I believe all that stuff."

"You don't have to, Fi, but for now can you just accept it's a possibility?"

"Well yes, I suppose so, because right at this moment I don't have any other explanation."

Again, they retreated into their own heads. Donna was lost in thoughts of the man being their guardian angel and how much comfort that gave her. She had always believed in life after death, and what she had witnessed as a nurse definitely confirmed that, but she had never had any experiences of her own. Until now that is. Knowing that the man was looking out for them was just amazing.

Fiona wasn't so convinced, although she had no explanation for his appearance. She reasoned that it was possible, although unlikely, that he could turn up in both Paris and here in Rhodes, but she couldn't explain why he was wearing exactly the same clothes and hadn't aged a bit. The fact that she couldn't explain his presence really gnawed away at her. She could usually fathom things out quite quickly, but not this time. On top of that she had Donna telling her to just accept it for what it was. Easier said than done, but right now she didn't have much choice.

"I think we ought to give him a name," said Donna.

"Mmm, really? What do you suggest – Angelo?"

"Yeah, I like that, but I was thinking more along the lines of Marcel, considering we first saw him in Paris."

"OK, if that's what you think then Marcel it is. I think we should try and get some sleep now."

"OK. Night, Fi; night, Marcel."

"Oh and one last thing," Donna said, five minutes later just as Fiona was dropping off to sleep.

CHAPTER 77

"Don't you think it's kind of fitting that we're here on *The Angel*?"

"Then we should definitely call him Angelo," replied a sleepy Fiona, *if we need to call him anything at all*, she thought.

They were just drifting off to sleep when Fiona had a sudden thought.

"Donna, we haven't looked at the photos you took earlier. Let's look now."

"Hang on and I'll get my phone."

Donna turned over in bed and retrieved her phone from the bedside table. Opening the camera she flicked back to the photos taken earlier that afternoon. She could hear Fiona prattling on in the background but she just looked in silence as she scrolled backwards and forwards on her phone.

"What's up, Don, did you get some good photos of him, our Angelo?"

"See for yourself," she said, as she handed the phone over to Fiona.

"Oh my God," said Fiona, "he's not in the boat."

Chapter 78

Thursday

After suggesting lunch in town, Nikos led the way to a beautiful taverna with outdoor seating and a magnificent sea view. They each ordered a Greek salad and a local beer. They talked as they ate and made plans for the rest of their holiday, although neither one of them would call it a holiday. But it was an adventure, and certainly something to tell their grandchildren.

Fiona and Donna wanted to collect their luggage from the hotel that afternoon. Matt was going to see Demetrios and Nikos needed to go back and rest. Pre-dinner drinks back on the *The Angel* later that evening would bring them all together again.

Nikos offered to get the girls a taxi to the hotel once they had finished eating, but they preferred to walk. They'd had little exercise over the past week and now they felt stronger it would do them good.

"Oh bloody hell," said Donna, as they walked through the hotel doors into reception, "it's the Winking Man Gang."

"Shit," replied Fiona, "can we avoid them?"

"Nope, he's spotted us and here they all come."

"Hello, you two. Where have you been? We've not seen you for ages and believe you and me, we have looked for you," Winking Man took the lead and treated them both to his biggest and best leering wink!

"Oh hello and yes, I'm sure you have," said Fiona. "But no, you wouldn't have seen us because we've been out and about having an adventure."

"Oh? What have you two been up to then?"

"Well, we've dealt with a dead body, been arrested for drug smuggling, met a billionaire shipping magnate and stayed on his yacht and been abducted, so not much really," Fiona said with a laugh.

"You two really crack me up," laughed Winking Man. His wife, no less sour looking after nearly a couple of weeks in the sun, took hold of him by his arm and dragged him away.

Fiona and Donna laughed as they collected their key from reception and made their way up to their room.

Packing didn't take long and they were soon back at reception ready to check out.

"But you have another five days yet," declared the receptionist.

"Yes, I know," said Fiona, "but we've made friends with a very influential and wealthy man and he has invited us to spend the rest of our holiday on his yacht. Oh and did I mention how extremely handsome he is? Tough choice I know, but I'm afraid the yacht won."

"I see," said the receptionist, rather stiffly as she completed the checkout procedure and gave them her 'farewell and do come again' parting shot.

Chapter 79

Fiona was looking forward to a nice relaxing evening, just the four of them. The relief when she saw Nikos and knew he was OK was enormous, and she was questioning why that should be. Was she tumbling into a relationship that could never be? She kept reminding herself that they only had a few more days of their holiday left before she had to return to her normal life, and the thought didn't fill her with joy. Her head told her to be cautious whilst her heart was telling her to live for the moment.

Donna, on the other hand, couldn't wait to get home. She missed Dave and her boys so very much, and there were moments during this holiday when she thought she would never see them again. If it hadn't been for Matt, she probably wouldn't ever see them again. She had much to be grateful to him for, and she really looked forward to getting to know him better over the next few days.

All four of them gathered on the middle deck.

"Ahoy there, permission to come aboard?" came a man's voice from the quay.

"Permission granted, come on up," said Nikos, smiling as he looked over the side.

They heard people climbing the steps and an older couple appeared on the terrace. Although his hair was grey, there was still a twinkle in the man's eyes, and his well-kept physique showed no signs of slowing down. The woman matched him in every way. Her hair was enhanced with a little colour from a bottle, and a few wrinkles around the eyes and mouth gave her age away, but her skin was flawless and her make-up applied perfectly. *Now that*, thought Donna, *is the way I want to grow old.* The couple oozed money in a completely classy, understated way.

"Everyone, please meet my parents," said Nikos as he made the introductions.

Ari and Tina were a handsome couple, and it was clear that Nikos had inherited the best genes from each of them. They were both gracious and chatted as if they had known everyone for ages. Obviously concerned for her son's wellbeing, Tina stood close, constantly touching his arm. She bore no malice as to the circumstances of his shooting, and they all spoke freely about the events of the past few days.

It had been such a lovely evening but after his parents left, Nikos apologised for their presence. He explained that he felt he couldn't say no to their visit as they both needed to see for themselves that their son really was OK. Although he would never call either of his parents as interfering or possessive, there was still a need on their part to ensure that all was well with him. Those feelings were entirely mutual, as he was the first to check on them if he hadn't heard from either for a couple of days.

"Oh Nikos, there really is no need to apologise at all. They are both lovely and of course they needed to see you. I'd be the same if it was one of my boys," said Donna, as she laid a hand on Nikos's arm. "You will always be your mum's baby."

"Anyway," chipped in Matt, "this is your boat, so you're entitled to have who you want here. We're just grateful that you have invited us all to stay for our last few days in Rhodes."

"It is my pleasure, and I have enjoyed every moment of your company. Even getting shot is worth the days spent together," Nikos replied as his eyes lingered over Fiona.

Chapter 80

Monday

With the final day of their holiday looming they made the most of their days lazing in the warm sunshine, and wonderful evenings getting to know each other better. They were forming lifelong friendships although none of them knew where that friendship would lead. Fiona and Nikos talked long into the night, and their relationship was heading far beyond friendship.

Matt and Donna laughed a lot as they shared stories of their past and hopes for the future. Donna's dreams were simple. She just wanted to be happy, dote on any grandchildren she may have, and share adventures with Fiona. Matt wished he could meet his special someone soon and settle down to a comfortable life. He would give up flying like a shot for the right person, but in the meantime he enjoyed jetting off around the world, seeing different places and meeting new people.

On their penultimate night in Rhodes, Nikos threw a party. Donna had mentioned that their holiday together was in celebration of their fiftieth birthdays so there was no better reason to celebrate. It was to be a modest affair by Nikos' standards, the guest list comprised mostly of people who the girls had got to know over the past couple of weeks.

Christos had asked Helena to join him, he knew she would never resist a party of this extravagance on a multi-million euro yacht. With a bit of luck, this would be exactly the type of reward that would keep her sweet throughout any future cases that required him to work extended hours.

Yiannis arrived alone. He was still very mixed up about what he wanted in life, but had decided to just go with the flow. After a heartfelt chat with Donna, who told him that what was meant for him would always find a way, he decided he could live with that. *What will be will be*, he thought.

Demetrios arrived and made a beeline for Donna and Fiona. Although Matt had told him they were safe and no actual harm had come to either of them, he needed to see for himself. He also wanted to see Matt, too, but was more than happy when he caught a glimpse of Yiannis chatting to Christos and Spiros and their wives.

When Lucas and Steve, accompanied by a couple of beautiful girls, arrived Fiona and Donna made their way across to them to thank them once again for all they had done. Nikos' parents were the last to board.

It was a cosy and intimate party. Conversation flowed and laughter rang out through the balmy night air. The twinkling lights strung around the yacht added atmosphere, and music played softly.

The crew had surpassed themselves with a never-ending supply of delicious food, and drink flowed well into the early hours. A big cake, adorned with fifty candles, was carried onto deck by Michalis and they all sang happy birthday; Donna and Fiona beamed with joy. The highlight of the evening was a live performance by an exceedingly good South African Motown tribute band who were currently doing the summer season of hotels in Rhodes. Nikos had heard that the band was very good and had paid well over the odds to persuade them to perform at a private party. He wasn't disappointed.

CHAPTER 80

"I'm sorry, Fiona," he said, holding her close as they danced to one of the slower numbers. "I tried to get Phil Collins, but he was already booked."

She threw her head back and laughed. She couldn't even remember telling him she liked Phil Collins. Perhaps Donna had let it slip.

"This is just perfect, Nikos, the best night I've ever had, certainly the best birthday party."

Fiona was stunned that someone would go to so much trouble to do something so wonderful just for her and her friend. This man was truly one in a million and she knew she would be stupid to let that go. But how their relationship could ever work was a huge problem.

Like all good things, the night had to end, and the partygoers started to take their leave and make their way home.

Donna and Matt caved into tiredness so said their goodnights, leaving Fiona and Nikos still talking quietly together.

"Do you know, Matt, I have a feeling that I'll not see Fiona until breakfast in the morning."

"I think you're right," he said, and kissing Donna on the cheek turned towards his own cabin.

Chapter 81

Wednesday

Just two weeks after their arrival on Rhodes it was time to go home. Neither of them could believe that so much had happened in such a short space of time. Their farewells were emotional. The crew of *The Angel* gathered on deck to see them off with hugs and kisses. Maria shed a few tears and made them promise to visit again, but without being abducted the next time. Nikos wanted to take them to the airport, but Fiona wouldn't let him. She didn't want an airport farewell. But he insisted that one of his drivers take them and help them with their luggage.

Saying goodbye to Nikos was hard, even for Donna. How do you thank a man who has been so generous, put himself out for you, even laid his life on the line for you? As much as Donna wanted to see Dave, she didn't want to say goodbye to Nikos. She and Matt said their goodbyes and made their way to the waiting car, giving Fiona and Nikos some privacy.

With her heart breaking Fiona clung to him, his arms wrapped tightly around her.

"Don't cry, *cara*, this is not a last goodbye. We will see each other again, I promise you that. I cannot let you go now that I have found you."

"Oh Nikos," sobbed Fiona. "I don't want to lose you either, but I can't see a way forward for us. I have a husband and children and I have to consider them too."

"I know, but never give up hope. Now you must go or you will miss your flight." Nikos pushed her away from him.

Finally, on board and settled into their seats, they prepared for the four-hour journey home. Their flight was uneventful. Donna was eager to see Dave, but Fiona was missing Nikos already. Although Matt had initially been booked on the same flight, the airline had sent a message a few days earlier asking if he would consider working his way back as they were short staffed. He readily agreed reasoning that he might as well get paid for a trip he was going to make anyway. It meant, of course, that he could keep them supplied in drinks and the inevitable pretzels. He stopped to check on them whenever he could. He was concerned about Fiona. With puffy eyes and a red nose, she looked so miserable.

She was subdued throughout the flight.

"You alright, sugar?" Donna asked.

"Yeah, I'll be alright," she replied. "I don't know why this is so hard for me, Donna, I've only known Nikos for a week or so, and yet here I am crying like a baby."

"I know, love, but he's made a big impact on you and he's given you something that nobody else has," said Donna. "I think you've got some serious thinking to do, lady."

"What do you mean?"

"Well," replied Donna, "it's blatantly clear to me you're not happy at home, and you're not happy with the life you have. So you have some choices to make, don't you?"

"Mmm, yes, I suppose so, but any choices I make will upset Jeremy," Fiona replied.

CHAPTER 81

"Yes, they probably will, but let's take him out of the picture for a moment. This is your life we're talking about and you deserve to be happy. So think about what would make you happy."

"Do you know the one thing I've wanted to do for a long time, Donna?"

"What's that, babe?"

"I would like to go back to work. I would like to be back using my brain, helping to solve crimes, helping people." Fiona was smiling for the first time since they left *The Angel*.

"Then why don't you do it?" Donna couldn't see the problem at all. If that's what Fiona wanted, then that's what she should do.

"Because it would upset Jeremy. He's never wanted me to work. From the day we got married he tried to get me to leave my job, but I hung on until I had James."

"Look, Fiona, I'm going to be quite blunt now. This is not Jeremy's life we're talking about, and he can't expect you to bow down to his every whim. Jeremy is a very selfish man, he's always had exactly what he's wanted, and he expects you to give in to him too. If you ask me, Jeremy is just plain abusive and I'm surprised you can't see it. He's bullying you. He's got you doing exactly what he wants you to do, and he doesn't give a toss whether it makes you happy or not."

"Oh Donna, it's just the way he's been brought up. He's always been used to getting exactly what he wanted, and he doesn't know how to be anything different."

"Bullshit. For Christ's sake, Fiona, stop making excuses for him. Nikos has had a very similar upbringing and they are poles apart; he only wants what will make you happy. That, my darling, is a sign of love." Donna was fed up with pussyfooting around her friend's marriage. It was about time she heard the truth.

Fiona went quiet. It was clear she was deep in thought and Donna left her to it. She only hoped that she would soon be ready to jump out of her comfort zone and make some life-changing decisions.

Chapter 82

Finally the plane touched down and made its way to the gate. Gathering up their hand luggage they waited until most passengers had disembarked so they could have a bit of extra time with Matt.

Tears flowed and promises were made to keep in touch and not leave it too long before they saw each other again. Many new friendships had been made during the holiday but none more important than Matt. They planned to do a Skype call the following weekend, and Donna knew she would spend the coming week looking forward to that very much.

Donna was getting increasingly impatient at the carousel, their luggage seemed to be taking forever. Why was coming home so much worse than the journey out? she wondered. She couldn't wait to see Dave and the boys. She was pleased to see that Fiona looked a little more cheerful, though. Maybe she had made some decisions during the flight. She knew her friend would tell her when the time was right.

After what seemed an age the conveyor belt started to move and luggage trudged its way round. The additional suitcase they each bought in Rhodes cost them extra at the airport as it far exceeded their luggage allowance, but they didn't care. Nikos, the lovely, generous man that he was, had insisted they take their new wardrobes home with them.

"Come now, what am I going to do with them?" he asked when they protested, but it didn't take either of them long to agree. Fiona was especially pleased as each item would remind her of him and their wonderful evenings and precious time spent together.

At last their suitcases appeared. Struggling to heave them all off the carousel and bumping them into the legs of fellow passengers constantly pushing forward to get as close to the conveyor belt as they could, they were very grateful to the young man next to them for lending a hand and piling them onto a trolley.

Heading for the green channel, they cleared through customs without incident and were through the doors to the Arrivals Hall. Donna was delighted to see Dave waiting for her. She thought Gavin might come, but this was just what she needed. She abandoned her trolley and flew into his waiting arms, crying tears of pure joy and relief that she was now safe and exactly where she needed to be.

Dave gave Fiona a big hug and asked if they could take her home.

"No, no, don't be silly, it's miles out of your way. But thank you, it's such a kind thought. But no, I have a taxi and in fact, that's him over there waving the placard with my name on."

Donna and Fiona hugged and said their goodbyes. Tears flowed again as neither of them wanted to leave the other.

"Message me when you get home, so I know you're safe," said Donna.

"Yes, I promise. You be safe. Dave, drive carefully."

They went their separate ways out of the airport, each of them missing the other already. This was the only downside of going on holiday together, the bereft feeling both had for days after saying goodbye. It was so painful and both wished the other lived closer.

Chapter 83

Finally Fiona opened her front door. She didn't want to be there but had no choice. This was never going to be the happy homecoming that Donna would be having with Dave and her boys. How she wished it was Nikos waiting for her instead of Jeremy.

She had seen Jeremy's car in the drive, so knew he must be home. She wasn't particularly looking forward to seeing him. She knew he would be cold and distant with her and she was fully aware that she was in for a rough ride. If only her children were home, at least she would have some joy in the house.

"Oh Fiona, it's you," he said coming into the hall, "you've finally come home then!" Fiona made a snap decision.

"Hello, Jeremy, yes, I'm home and I want a divorce."

Acknowledgments

Thanks to my special friend Pat Hesketh, for listening to my ramblings, helping to guide me in the right direction, reading the draft manuscript, pointing out my numerous errors and for keeping me going when I was about to give up.

Thanks to my bestie Gill Moss, for coming up with the initial idea that shaped the series. I thought it was stupid, but you planted the seed. Thank you also for believing in me when I didn't believe in myself.

Thanks to my editor, Helen Baggott, who helped shape the book, make it readable and for telling me when things just didn't work.

Special thanks to my family for your continual support and encouragement, and endless cups of tea.

Finally, I am grateful to you for buying and reading this book. I hope you enjoyed it.

Also By

Thanks for joining Donna and Fiona on their first holiday experience, and the first in the Innocents Abroad Crime Series.

If you enjoyed the book, and have a moment to spare, I would really appreciate a short review on Amazon.

The pair's next holiday experience is on the way. A Sardinian Misfortune should be published Summer 2022.

While you're waiting why not download three FREE short stories, each featuring Donna and Fiona, from my website.

Also by Elaine Collier

Once Bitten, Twice Prepared

The Bigger Picture

Keep up to date with Elaine Collier on her website www.elainecollier.com.

About the Author

Elaine Collier started writing during the Covid pandemic in 2020 and is the author of two non-fiction books about her own personal life experiences.

Having discovered a passion for writing she subsequently turned to fiction. *A Greek Misadventure* is the first in a series of the holiday adventures of two best friends who always manage to fall into some sort of crime. The second in the series is due out in 2022.

She writes with humour, insight, and is very down to earth.

Elaine's first book, *Once Bitten, Twice Prepared*, written during the height of the Covid pandemic in 2020/21, tells her story of her two different experiences with breast cancer. Her second book, *The Bigger Picture*, takes the reader through her spiritual journey.

Elaine lives in Oxfordshire, UK, with her non-blood family and a hyperactive and very verbal kitten, Dexter. After several different careers, including running her own business in mind, body and spirit training, she now writes full time.

"Life is a journey and who knows what will come next, but it's up to each of us to make it as exciting as possible."

Printed in Great Britain
by Amazon